I0520261

# HYPERPOWERS

Third Flatiron Anthologies
Volume 5, Book 16, Summer 2016

**Guest Edited by Bascomb James**
**Cover Art by Keely Rew**

# Hyperpowers
Third Flatiron Anthologies
Volume 5, Summer 2016

Published by Third Flatiron Publishing
Bascomb James, Guest Editor
Juliana Rew, Publisher

**Discover other titles by Third Flatiron:**

**License Notes**

**www.thirdflatiron.com**

# Contents

*****~~~~~***

# Editor's Note

by Bascomb James

Welcome to the *Hyperpowers* anthology, the 16th volume of speculative fiction published by Third Flatiron Publications. When Publisher Juliana Rew offered me my choice of assignments, I was drawn to the *Hyperpowers* anthology because of its theme—Military Science Fiction and Space Opera, arguably the most maligned yet popular sub-genre within the speculative fiction pantheon. Many people believe the overall popularity of this story-form is due, in part, to the success of movie and television franchises including *Star Wars, Star Trek, Babylon 5, Stargate, Battlestar Galactica, Farscape, Firefly, The Expanse*, and *Guardians of the Galaxy*. While that may be true, the print-world has embraced space opera since its inception in the early 1900s. From 1982 to 2002, the Hugo Award for best science fiction novel was commonly given to a space opera nominee. Not that it marked the end of an era; Ann Leckie's space opera *Ancillary Justice* won the 2014 Hugo Award in addition to the Nebula Award, the Arthur C. Clarke Award, and the BSFA Award. Whether you love it or loathe it, I firmly believe good space opera embodies the best features of SF—dramatic, large-scale adventures focusing on character, world building, and plot action.

*Hyperpowers* opens with William Huggins's "Grid Drop." In this story, William introduces us to a fallow Earth and a cadre of eco warriors working to keep the remaining humans from recreating ecological mistakes of the past. Dan Koboldt's fast-paced "Dirt Moon" brings us another group of grunts who battle gravoid-like beasts that move rapidly through the dirt and take their victims from below. The space navy takes center stage in "Outer Patrol" by E. J. Shumak. In this timeless story, patrol crews discover the unsavory secret behind recurring alien attacks in the sector.

When I think about artificial intelligence, my mind quickly wanders to the sentient beings depicted in *Blade Runner*, the soulless AI assassins from the *Terminator* franchise, and to the noble BOLO units described in Keith Laumer's classic SF tales. In "Pre-emptive Survivors," Martin Clark introduces us to naval intelligence unit Polyakov Seventeen, a covert AI "sanitation" unit who has no problem snipping loose ends to further its cause. And finally, John M. Campbell brings us "The Silicates," a tale about sentient AI units hunted by a space miner for their salvage value. But the silicates are tricksy, so very tricksy.

Two authors show us the lighter side of military science fiction. In Erik B. Scott's "Duck and Cover," cheesy public service announcements are instrumental in staving off an alien invasion, and in "Kill the Coffee-Boilers," Robert Walton introduces us to a stuffy academic soldier leading a training simulation on an alien planet.

Poignant takes on future military conflict are the darlings of the SF community right now, and this anthology includes several poignant tales for your enjoyment. Sam Bellotto, Jr. brings us "Symphony in First Contact, Hostile," an account of an alien invasion and its emotional aftermath. The story is told within a symphonic structure. In "The Mytilenian Delay," Neil James Hudson spotlights the human conflict within a warship after it receives orders to destroy a heavily populated planet. Should they countermand the order? Author Noel Ayers provides a modern twist on a classic tale about a military veteran irrevocably changed by the war in "Yesterday's Weapon." Can this soldier ever feel normal again?

Writing space opera in less than 3,000 words is incredibly difficult, but our authors demonstrated they were up for the challenge. In Jonathan Shipley's "Between

Two Heartbeats," a quick-thinking young space trader uses a Highborn Princess to escape corrupt planetary officials. A solar miner encounters aliens who want her precious exotic matter cargo in Elliotte Rusty Harold's story, "Claim Jumpers." Mark Rookyard shares a thoughtful tale about an Imperial Chief of Staff who wants to forget everything and enjoy life for a while in "Dreaming Empire." "Child of Soss" is an anthropological morality play by Brandon L. Summers. In this story, an insect-like alien grows to respect a human refugee. To round out this category, author K. S. Dearsley shares her story, "Alien Dreams," an interesting tale about alien explorers who encounter a spacecraft carrying a golden data disk. The disk contains an ancient prayer.

"Grins and Gurgles" is a regular humor feature in the Third Flatiron anthologies, presenting as it were, a literary palette-cleanser after a meal of delectable speculative fiction. In this volume, we've included a flash fiction story from Art Lasky. "I've Got the Horse Right Here. . ." is a cautionary tale about a man who saves a fairy and is granted one wish.

As I wrap up these notes, I must confess my surprise and pleasure when Juliana Rew first asked me to edit this volume. This is her baby, and fans of the series will note that my editorial preferences don't perfectly overlap with hers. We are, after all, different people. For these reasons, I am extremely grateful to Juli for her trust and for giving me this exciting opportunity. I also want to extend my thanks to all the authors who answered the call for stories. I had to make tough choices, eliminating some really good stories in order to create a balanced and varied lineup. To you, the reader, I offer this outstanding selection of short speculative fiction. It truly represents the best of the best.

Happy reading!
Bascomb James
April 2016

# Grid Drop

by William Huggins

Hardfall woke her.

Celeste blinked, checked chrono. The shuttle shook hard through the lower reaches of the mesosphere—200 and sinking fast. She nodded, took a long drag from her water line. Mikio, Min, and Pyetr woke as well and sipped, then partnered to check seals on their suits from toes to neck. Mikio took an extra second to tuck Celeste's long dark hair into the neckline, nimble fingers whose touch Celeste knew well. Everyone sealed helmets, fired suit diagnostics, and fastened rifles tightly against lower backs, snug below the light 'chute bags. The shuttle shook once more, hard, then plunged forward in a smooth and deep fall. Celeste's faceplate flashed green, twice.

"DT8-4, outbound." She fired the link, and a triple matrix flashed on faceplates, tracking for all of them. A door slipped open to her left, and she stepped toward it.

"Luck," the tinny voice came from the cockpit.

Without responding, Celeste stepped out, angled herself in a steep dive, fellow commandos falling close behind her. Arms to her side, she tracked progress across the faceplate, angling against the winds to nudge slight course corrections as needed. Kilometers ticked off in the upper left corner. She watched the team adjust behind her as she shifted, perfect tandem though it had been months since they'd made a drop.

Freedom, ah—the pure freedom of falling.

*Drops so rare these days,* she thought. *So few grids left.*

Fifteen minutes until dawn. The deep darkness below loomed like a bottomless pit, as if they were falling through pure space and not toward the dark gravity well of the world below. Hard to believe two centuries earlier most of the mass would have been lit up like a control board, networks of electric light spanning entire continents. No more. Two hundred years of Fallowing had pulled all evidence of historic human activities from the surface, removing everything non-organic the Dirty Ones created, from the smallest article to the largest city—the work of generations, leaving the planet to heal.

*Mostly,* Celeste thought.

Some resisted the Authority's vision and took to the wilds to live. Most were left to their own devices so long as they did not violate Authority standards. Indigenous peoples who returned to traditional lifeways were given a wide berth. It was not they who had taken the planet to the brink of ecological catastrophe. But any who kept up some of the poor practices of the Dirty Ones were visited by a scattering of teams, one of which Celeste and her crew comprised. They fell toward one such place now.

*Fools.*

She steeled herself. She let the cold air and chill wind wrap around her, cool the heart she'd need for the action. It was all too easy to take in the human component, to let compassion for a small group slip in when the larger Fallowing had to be considered. The healing that took root below her, that swept away the malignancy of five centuries of abuse, took precedence over other concerns. She found it hard to see how anyone could fail to see that simple fact: the contract with all life the Dirty Ones abrogated, the Fallowing repaired.

They fell, invisible, numbers descending swiftly. She kept her attention on the boards, tracking distance, fall rate, the spread of the team. But part of her attention she let drift right, knowing what was coming—the best part of this or any drop, if you timed them properly. She tracked the minutes, made the calculations in her head with no need for the complex algorithms that spilled across her faceplate, until the event began to unfold. You could watch it from the *Rise Against* in orbit far above, but here, in the air over the world—ah, this was the place to truly see it happen.

*Magic*, she thought. Not that she believed in those ancient stories, any more than the other myths of that old world. But no other word fit her experience. While that dark world spun, pulling them down and along with it, suddenly a crimson explosion sprang over the horizon, spilling across the darkness like warmth. The world turned showy suddenly, as if a curtain fled, chased by a light determined to expose everything. The sight never failed to fill her with awe. As if from nowhere, the world filled slowly with forests, patches of open water, hills, mountains, valleys, and large empty swaths of grassland and prairie.

All empty, open, wild—no longer marred by humankind.

*Mostly*, she thought again.

She drifted through a small layer of cloud, made a slight course correction. The team moved with her. She watched the morning unfold below, falling toward a deep patch of forest with an open glade. Closer—she could see buildings now, with glimmers of light flashing along their rooftops.

"Now." She tapped a key on her chest and felt the familiar snap as the 'chute opened. She caught a crossing thermal and guided herself expertly down over the village still quiet and sleeping. No movement anywhere in the spaces between dwellings. She counted twenty-five structures as she crossed and landed softly in a small open area to the north. She squatted and waited until the other three joined her on the ground, then unbelted the 'chutes. They wrapped and stowed them quickly and quietly, set them together in a pile. Each freed a rifle, softly opening its three sections and testing power. She looked up. Radios would stay on for emergencies; all other communication would be hand signs now, and she watched three flash—*check.*

They moved toward the buildings in silence, above them a sky blue with light clouds scattered high above. Waking birdsong carried in the morning stillness. The tread across uneven ground always surprised Celeste at first. She smiled slightly in wonder, enjoying the odd feeling of uneven surfaces underfoot, the strange look and sensation of morning dew, spitting reflections back at the new sun. Boots slid some, but everyone on the team was experienced and quickly adapted. As they reached the village's edge, she flashed a hand signal to Pyetr, and he moved away to the right.

They stepped between two squat buildings, wooden edges fraying. Poorly insulated wires hung low between the buildings, winding their way through the village with varying states of tautness. The buildings seemed loosely organized around a central core. She flashed a signal, and Min slipped to the left, silent even over the smooth rocks that coated the ground now.

Celeste lowered her carbine and checked the charge again. Full. She'd never had to use it, but training never let her forget regs. To her right, she saw Mikio do the same, nodded in approval. Two greens on the faceplate represented Min and Pyetr. All well. Celeste and Mikio stepped forward into the central area.

The small space opened into what was mostly a circle, with benches, tables, a water trough, and a bell

14

arranged in the center. A tall pole held a light that was off now, a battery at the base fed by an exposed line. Dangerous. She followed the line to the closest building and saw the gleam of the solar panel reflecting the sun, a last bit of dew burning off its base. Most of the homes had panels on them, angled as much as they could on the southern faces, catching the most sun over the course of the year at this latitude.

The battery at the base of the pole was far too small to charge the village at night. *This light*, Celeste thought, *communal meeting area*. She was touched at the thought, the village and its denizens outside under the stars, telling stories or singing songs or practicing whatever religion they still might have. Perhaps a tinge of jealousy, envy—that they had had this time, even if illegal, to stay in touch with the world, know it in a way she never would.

"Battery," Mikio said softly, breaking into her thoughts.

Celeste made a cutting motion with her hand.

Mikio nodded and fired her carbine at its lightest setting, searing the dark box at the pole's base and kicking it away. She lifted the rifle and fired at the small bulb, shattering it. Hard to imagine they would have another. Celeste cocked her head. Mikio shrugged, probably smiling behind the dark faceplate. Celeste knew her partner, yes—suited and not.

Min appeared with a purposeful, satisfied air, rifle at the ready, scanning the huts as she walked. Nothing. No movement. Celeste found that slightly odd. The team worked silently, yes, skilled as any, but with the morning now past its inception someone should have been about. She heard not even movement within the buildings. She raised a hand—*hold*.

The three women spun and faced outward, waiting for signs of life. The stillness continued, windless, light sounds from the forest pressing against the clearing. The wildness this last pocket of civilization held at bay, which would be consumed when their work was done.

Pyetr still green, still moving. She wondered where he was, why Min had made her circuit so quickly—

Movement to her left, and she turned gracefully, carbine raised, catching a grey-haired woman whose wrinkled face twisted in shock. *Elder,* Celeste thought instantly. She lifted the rifle, and the woman's hands rose into the air. She pointed to the nearest bench, and the woman made her way there slowly, taking her time to sit, evident pain moving across her body in the action. She held an earthenware mug in one hand. Celeste held a finger to her faceplate, for silence.

"Mikio, water," she said quietly. She and Min covered the homes as Mikio took the mug, filled it from the trough, and took it back to the old woman, who took a deep drink.

"We never thought you would come," she said, and sipped again.

Celeste shook her head and raised a finger to her faceplate again. The woman looked down and contemplated the mug.

Mikio retook her position, and they waited, signs of life gradually appearing. They guided the villagers to the water, shadowing them with their weapons as they filled mugs and took seats on benches. The day warmed. No fires, though Celeste was sure there had to be wood stocked somewhere. Even with solar assistance for heat, winters were rugged here. Perhaps Pyetr found the place and was documenting it. His light still burned bright green. Where was he? She didn't want to risk a communication if he was in hiding. But if he was, why hadn't he coded to red?

After several minutes went by without anyone else appearing, Celeste stepped forward. She counted thirty-seven people, twelve of them children, most of whom looked filthy and emaciated, as did everyone else. *Not a thriving community, this.* All dressed in rags or hides, animal skins and the like, patched and sewed over many times. Bare feet, now—though doubtless foot coverings hid inside the hovels somewhere, held back for use in the colder months. In spite of herself she couldn't help but be impressed: they had held on these many generations, making what lives they could. She lowered her carbine.

"You are the Elder?"

The older woman nodded, looked to her right at a man of indeterminate age, hairless, deep lines in his face. "And him."

He looked up, sunken eyes alit with fear, perhaps anger. Celeste had seen her share of both. "*Evil,*" he hissed.

Celeste addressed the group. "You may have heard tales of us." No few nodded. "We respect your Elders, villagers. They will give you their counsel. Let me give you ours: we come as representatives of the Fallowing, to offer you lives of service to a greater good, to undo what our ancestors did to this world, to bring you health and prosperity."

The old man raised himself on shaky legs. "You come only with *evil!* Blasphemy!"

The woman reached for him. "Harold—"

He pushed her hands away. "They come, my friends, my family, to take our *lives.*" He stepped forward and pointed at the pole. "Already our light is gone. They will take more, everything: our village, our homes. Burn them. This. . . this is *our* land, *our* world. And you would take us from it and give it back to things that do not even reason."

Celeste nodded. "Yes. Your village will no longer exist. We will take what can be recycled and burn the rest. It has no place here. *You.* . . have no place here. No longer. You may stay, if that is your choice. Or you may come with us, when the scavenger appears, and we will give you new lives in service to the Fallowing."

"In service to *evil*!" He shook a fist. "I will not go with you. Ever! If I were but younger, and if I had a weapon—"

"You would die futilely," Celeste snapped, suddenly out of patience with the old fool. She turned to the woman. "Is this the entire village?"

The woman shook her head. "Two in the sickhouse. And another, somewhere. . . "

Celeste thought suddenly of Pyetr—but he was green, and too good to be trapped by a villager. She hoped.

She clicked to long mode. "DT8-4, sending coordinates. Possibly 40 live, all ages, two ill. Not thirty structures."

The response was quick: "SCA-54-44, prenotified. On refinery wipe east, reassigning. 20 minutes, DT8-4."

"Aye." She closed the line, turned again to the villagers. "Speak among yourselves, take what counsel you will. We can take you all, if all are willing." She looked at the Elders. The man sat with his face in his hands, the woman stared at her listlessly. "Think of the children and the ill. As well as yourselves."

The villagers moved to make a circle around their Elders. Then Mikio cried out and fell to her knees, grabbing her chest, carbine falling to the ground. The villagers screamed and tightened in a mass. The old woman stood on the bench shouting. Min spun, looking for what had hit Mikio. Celeste fought every instinct to leap to Mikio, kept her head up and swung her carbine back and forth, searching the houses. "Mikio?"

"Fine," she said, gasping for breath. "Maybe a rib." She picked up her carbine with one hand and ran the other over her suit. "No puncture." She reached down and lifted a shaft from the ground, sharp-edged on the front, fletched with feathers on the back. Celeste shook her head. *Arrows? What fools.*

"Go," Mikio hissed, raising herself to her feet and holding her rifle in both hands. "Find him before he hurts someone else."

"Min?"

Min held her carbine up, facing into a row of houses behind the trough. "In there."

"Cover me," Celeste said. She went to move forward but stopped. From the shadows of a house, a huge boy stepped, arms behind his head. Pyetr appeared behind him, carbine at his back, a huge crossbow slung over his shoulder. He pushed the boy to the center, made him sit at the pole. Then he set down his carbine while Celeste covered him. He swiftly broke the old weapon into pieces.

"Have mercy," the old man said, finally looking up. "We need that—"

Pyetr fiercely threw the wooden base away and reclaimed his carbine. "I'm very clear what you need it for, old one."

Celeste had never heard quiet anger burning behind his words before. It worried her. "Pyetr—"

"If you will," he said.

Celeste turned to Min, gave a quick sign—*cover*. She stepped past the boy with his lowered head and followed Pyetr. They moved quickly between several homes, turning twice, until they came to a smaller building with a slanted roof and steel smokestack, made entirely of wood. At its side clung an ancient battery, the lifeblood of the village. The door hung slightly ajar on poor hinges. Pyetr stopped.

"Cover?"

He shook his head. "It's clear. I've seen. Once is enough."

She opened the door and let the light of morning fill the space, then leapt back. Her heart pounded, and her vision went dark for a moment, even from that brief sight, like something from the old vids: the stench, the matted, hanging forms, bloody hooks and blades, and bench. In a

19

decade of drops, she had never seen anything like it. But it made sense, she thought, as she let the anger wash away and cooled herself—it made sense. *No gardens, no sign of agriculture—but this. . .*

"Burn it," she said.

"Aye." She heard the carbine activate and the smell of smoke as she walked away. She half-ran back to the circle, found all to be as she left it. One of the villagers asked to give the boy some water, and she approved. She knelt next to Mikio, who sat now, carbine across her lap. Celeste touched her shoulder, and Mikio nodded, closed her hand over hers for a moment, then gripped her weapon again.

"Five minutes," Celeste said. "Maybe less. Will you come with us?"

The old man rose. "Some will. Some will not. I will not." He waved a hand at the smoke rising over the village. "Though you have killed us now, taking our food."

"You had no right to take those lives."

"So you say. You who worship these things as if they were people, but *we* are your people! *We* are people! Do you not see that?" He waved his arms. "Do you not see us for what we are?"

"Yes," Celeste said. "And for what you could be. Choose as you will."

Pyetr returned, and they led the villagers to the clearing to the north. The wind blew their way, and the smell of burning flesh choked them for a moment until it shifted. As it did, the scavenger appeared, flying low across the treetops. It settled on the far side of the clearing. A door opened, and two crews spilled forth in small wheeled vehicles. They raced into the village. The old man moved as if to stop them, but the woman held him, and he rested his head on her shoulder. They moved slowly away from the group.

## Grid Drop

A young girl came and touched Celeste's leg, feeling the strength of the fabric that covered her. She looked up, bright green eyes through black tangled hair. She smiled. "I will. . . come. Food. Please, food."

Celeste touched her head. "We have more than enough for you."

Another girl approached. "I will be like you, do what you do."

"Let us hope you will never have to."

Others came and gathered around, and she had Min and Mikio led them to the scavenger, Mikio limping and obviously in pain. Pyetr waited until a small vehicle passed with the two ill villagers, then took the last, leaving Celeste to wait. The crews cleaned the village in less than an hour, too good at their work by far, scouring the panels and wires, the fallen central battery and the burned one on the village's eastern edge. Truly there was little that was useful anymore. Then they set fires as they drove back to the scavenger, and the village began to burn.

Celeste moved up to the six remaining figures, all old but for the boy. She never knew what to say to them, those who would not come: that their community was failing, they were starving, they were doomed? They knew all that already. At least they had the children—the children always came. She slung the carbine over her shoulder. "One last chance." She appealed to the young man with an open hand. "For you, of all of them. You have no future here." But he simply looked down and did not answer.

She walked away, folding her carbine as she went—she no longer needed it. She crossed the grass quickly. The door slid shut behind her as she boarded, and she heard the engines rise. She did not want to go see those who had come with them yet—could not. She knew Mikio would be in the care of a medical crew now, beginning the healing journey. She waited for the scavenger to lift—per her ritual she could not move until

21

then. She looked at the small group gathered on the grass below, forced herself to watch, to remind herself of the mixed truths in what she did. Six more added. As always she could see them: the faces that lined up over the years with the same look as they lifted away—though they never saw hers, like her parents when they sent her away, those faces would never leave her.

###

## About the Author

William Huggins lives, writes, and works in the desert southwest with his wife, daughter, and three dogs. He spends a great deal of time exploring wild places. Besides a previous story with Third Flatiron, his work has appeared at *Another Realm, Expanded Horizons, Texas Books in Review,* and wearewildness.com/blog.

*****~~~*****

# Between Two Heartbeats

by Jonathan Shipley

"Edric, watch out!" Calem yelled from across the bridge as a sleek yacht zipped across their orbit approach on a fast collision course.

His nephew yelped and swerved out of the way. "That idiot pilot! What the hell was he—"

"Let it go!" Calem snapped abruptly as he took in more data from the scans. "And be thankful."

"What?"

"That's a royal yacht, lad. Always has right of way. Just thank the stars you didn't collide with it. Would have been first degree treason."

Calem watched his nephew absorb that information, watched the anger dissolve with a shudder. The boy might be brash, but at least he could recognize a disaster about to bite his arse. That was an essential survival skill for any free-trader. . . that and a nose for politics. Not an attraction to politics, you understand, but a nose that could smell the rotting corpse of intrigue from a distance was worth its weight in any currency.

He was getting a whiff of something now. Royal yachts didn't just happen in Degan airspace. Dega had little to nothing to do with Throneworld and the Empire and the high-and-mighty Highborn race that dominated everything on the galactic event horizon. And yet a royal yacht. He sniffed the data a little more closely and frowned. Not just any royal yacht, it seemed, but the

*Kishone*, personal vessel of the Princess Royale, arguably the second most powerful Highborn after the High Prince himself, which made the two bitter enemies. This was starting to feel about as safe as a herd of stampeding kakra. Calem's nose said to break orbit and find another market for the hold full of urridom. Unfortunately, that wasn't possible. They were sputtering back home on empty after a long, but productive trading cycle.

Calem sighed and dipped his little corsair into the atmosphere for a surface landing. They would just have to be careful.

The landing was fine, the docking and refueling was fine. . . but something was still off. Calem sensed it out on the tarmac and felt it like a punch in the gut as soon as he and Edric stepped into the port concourse. Droves of passengers coming and going to the shuttle transport docks, the cargo sleds negotiating through the masses—that was normal, but security wasn't. Four times the number of spaceport guards usually assigned to a shift, he noted with growing unease.

Beside him, Edric shifted uneasily. "Is this a sweep for contraband?" he muttered, his eyes also on the guards.

Calem shrugged. Surely that would have been too great a coincidence. "More likely something to do with the Princess Royale," he finally said. "The extra guards could be just for show."

But his nose didn't believe it. The smell of danger was too great. His was a one-ship operation. Limited cargo space meant fast, high-risk runs of edge merchandise that sold for a quick profit. Edge merchandise was legal, but right on the border of being contraband. This trip it had happened—the cargo he and Edric had brought back had been re-categorized in their absence. Urridom slices were now on the contraband list by order of the Dega Import Authority. They'd learned that too late to do anything about it. Oh, they could have jettisoned the urridom in the upper atmosphere, but that was very much a last resort. No cargo meant no profit, and no profit meant starting from scratch to raise fresh capital for another venture.

And now all these security guards. The presence of extra guards might have nothing to do with contraband, but Edric was already jumpy, and Calem wasn't feeling so secure himself. The line between free trader and smuggler was already thin. A mistake at this point could mean a couple of years in prison.

"Uncle."

Calem tensed at the urgency in Edric's voice, then slowly turned his head. On one of the overhanging balconies, Harl Joban, Chief of the Import Authority, was enjoying a leisurely java with someone in the burgundy company colors of the TransStellar Trade Combine. That wasn't good. TransStellar made a practice of squeezing free traders out of business whenever the opportunity arose, but the corporation had been at odds with the Import Authority over tariffs for as long as Calem could remember. If that dispute was now resolved, the situation was worse than bad. Corruption in the Import Authority was legendary, and TransStellar had deep pockets.

Not taking his eyes off the two men, Calem caught hold of Edric's arm. "Go back to town, find your mother, and head for the country. I'll finish matters here." The situation—the sudden prohibition of urridom, the chummy scene on the balcony, the extra guards—was starting to smell too strongly for his nose to ignore. Improbable though it was, it had the feel of a trap. Harl Joban liked those kinds of games.

Edric's expression hardened, but he didn't argue, just moved off toward the exit ramp. For that, Calem was thankful. The boy could be willful at times—not a bad trait in a free trader—but willful at this moment could spell disaster.

A hand on his shoulder broke Calem's concentration. A guard in the blue and gray of the Import

Authority gestured for him to follow. Calem's eyes darted around, looking for a convenient opening in the crowd where he could disappear.

"Don't bother. You wouldn't get halfway to the exit." Harl Joban, still wiping a trace of java from his mouth with a gold-edged napkin, sauntered up. "A *routine* security sweep turned up contraband in your cargo hold, trader. Unless you have amazing evidence to offer, your case will be dealt with summarily."

"Entrapment," Calem protested. "Urridom wasn't contraband when we left. You have no right to prosecute retroactively."

Harl Joban gave an elaborate shrug. "Justice is a slow process here on Dega. And I am fully empowered to impose interim sentences on smugglers. You'll have your day in court. . . in a decade or two."

At least Edric got away, Calem told himself. The boy was smart enough to—

His hope soured as two guards appeared, dragging Edric back to Joban. So the trap was complete.

"Cargo. . . confiscated," Harl Joban announced as he punched in codes on his datapad to make it so. "Ship. . . impounded. Smugglers—oh, excuse me—free traders. . . remanded to district prison until further notice. I believe, gentlemen, that concludes our business."

"It's not fair!" Edric protested. "We did nothing wrong!"

The words rang strangely loud. . . louder than they should have in a crowd that size.

"We're not smugglers. . ." Calem insisted, then fell silent as he realized the unnatural cessation of background noise.

Calem knew even before he caught sight of the ripple in the crowd. The Highborn princess. Where a moment before the concourse floor had been a press of bodies, now a track opened as people backed out of the path of the royal party. Those closest to the way bowed or genuflected; others simply cast down their eyes.

*And technically Dega isn't even part of the Empire,* Calem thought to himself. But the will of a Highborn, once aroused, overrode all political boundaries. The Princess Royale was merely a guest on a world with only indirect trade ties to Throneworld with its thousands of subservient star systems. But no Highborn was "merely" anything. Governments fell for giving offense to these star princes; governments fell for merely attracting the wrong sort of attention. If only Dega's government would attract such attention.

The princess's party was small—only herself and half a dozen Stedren warriors—but it seemed larger as it crossed the concourse. The Stedrens wore full body armor, polished to mirror brightness, and the princess wore the traditional flowing cloak of cloth-of-gold, its train lapping and curling in rhythm to its master's stride like some semi-sentient creature. And surrounding both cloak and wearer was a nimbus. Only a very light nimbus, Calem noted. The Highborn must not deem Dega important enough to generate a full Nimbus of Power. And for that they could all be thankful.

The crowd dipped in waves as people bowed. Suddenly Harl Joban was bowing as well, and his guards. Calem realized the path of the procession was taking the party close to where he was standing. He genuflected, clawing at Edric to bring him down, too. The trick was not to attract attention.

But Edric broke free and dashed forward to kneel directly in the path of the glowing personage.

A collected gasp escaped the crowd, but faster even than the exhalation two Stedrens rushed forward, blasters pressed against Edric's temples. Calem looked away, expecting to hear the soft whine of the blasters discharging into the boy's head. But instead he heard conversation.

27

"I seek an audience with the princess," Edric murmured. If the concourse hadn't been deathly still, the words never would have carried.

Calem stared at the scene in growing disbelief. He had thought the move a suicide attempt on Edric's part, a desperate decision to die quickly rather than in little pieces in prison. But no, he actually wanted an audience.

The long train of the golden robe flicked back and forth like a prehensile tail, betraying more of the Highborn's indecision than anything that might cross that cold mask of a face. Stealing a glance at the face to confirm this thought, Calem found he could tell nothing. Pale as marble with hair with eyes of glittering gold, the princess could be considered beautiful in a cold, god-like way, but there was nothing human in her expression.

Calem's gaze drifted back to the train of the cloak. That was the only clue what would come next. That was where the Stedrens would read the response of their mistress, for she surely she would not deign to speak to underlings and natives. At least the cloak had not swatted Edric aside. That was a good sign.

Even watching closely, Calem missed whatever subtle sign passed between Highborn and Stedrens, for suddenly a warrior yanked Edric to his feet and was pulling him forward toward the luxury shuttle lounge, where he opaqued the walls.

The Highborn had granted Edric an audience? Even seeing it right before his eyes, Calem could not believe it. It defied all protocol. It would lead nowhere, of course, he told himself. Edric had merely caught the princess's fleeting attention. Thirty seconds and she would be bored with the plea and bored with the boy.

But that was still thirty seconds.

He turned to face Harl Joban, who stood staring in confusion after the receding procession. "Perhaps we could negotiate," Calem said, his voice sounding calmer than his wildly beating heart.

"You have *nothing* to negotiate!" Harl Joban snapped. "This changes nothing in the indictment."

But Calem could hear the edge of fear on his words. This was a man who had nothing to gain and everything to lose by this sudden turn. Yes, governments fell when Highborn got involved.

"No? I can think of many changes that could come from this. Five words, perhaps, from the lips of a certain personage: 'The Import Authority offends me.' And how will the Degan Presidium respond to such an utterance, do you suppose? Come, tell me, Joban, you know these people better than I. How will your superiors respond?"

Harl Joban's face dissolved into a mask of fury, and Calem feared he had pushed too hard. He had touched the hidden terror that Joban and his guards and TransStellar must all be feeling at this moment. Those five words or anything like them would spell the end of the entire Dega trade structure as it currently existed. The Presidium would, of course, fall all over itself, summarily disbanding the Import Authority to show that the offensive agency had been dealt with.

Harl Joban took a breath and regained a measure of control. "She will never utter those words. Far more likely that your fool nephew will say the wrong thing and have his face blown off."

Calem inwardly agreed, but couldn't afford to yield the point. "All things are possible. The question is, how much is it worth to the Import Authority to have one particular possibility removed? If I were to go down to the shuttle lounge and signal my nephew that all is well, for instance. What is that worth to you?"

Unlike the Highborn, Harl Joban wore his emotions on his face. Several were currently warring.

"I'm too small a prize for the risk," Calem added. "TransStellar may hate free traders, but it would hate worse a trade agency here on Dega that was less, shall we

29

say, cooperative. Your corporate friends will not cushion your fall."

Joban gave an exasperated sigh. "None of that is going to happen. Find passage offworld today. Take the boy."

"In my own ship."

"But the urridom remains confiscated as contraband."

Calem shrugged agreement. He probably couldn't win that one, not with Joban planning to sell the stuff on the black market for personal profit. "All charges dropped," he counteroffered. "And no charge for the current fueling."

"But find another trade route. Your business is no longer welcome on Dega."

So, Joban could report back to TransStellar that one more free trader was out of the picture. "I'm gone," Calem nodded. "Clear me for takeoff. Five minutes." He waited until Joban transmitted the clearance codes.

As Calem started toward the lounge, his mind jumped from the improbable bargain he had managed to pull off with Joban to the impossible task of interrupting the Highborn mid-discussion. But he still had forty feet before dealing with that. Or maybe—

He slowed, unnerved by a new thought. Maybe Harl Joban was counting on the Stedrens to finish off a pushy free trader who stuck his head in where protocol didn't permit. More convolutions ran through his mind as he approached the doorway, each worse than the last. *Steady now*, he told himself.

No Stedrens on duty at the doorway, he noticed. That just meant they were all inside, blasters just as ready as ever. But Edric had survived *his* breach of protocol. Maybe this Highborn was unusually compassionate. Calem let the thought roll around a moment, then decided he was arriving at early senility. No one ever paired the words "compassionate" with "Highborn."

He stole a glance at Harl Joban, who was still watching intently from across the concourse, took a breath, and walked through the doorway.

No Stedrens. No Highborn. Edric knelt in the middle of the floor, looking a little dazed. He was alone and barefoot. His boots lay on the floor in front of him. What?

Calem's brain kicked back in with a vengeance. "Come on, son. We're cleared for takeoff in five, all charges dropped. I managed a deal with Joban that promised your lady friend wouldn't demolish his career. I'd really like to be offworld before certain parties realize she's gone and we have nothing left to bargain with."

Edric looked, if anything, more confused but pulled on his boots, and followed his uncle out the exterior door to the docking area. Their clearance held— Calem thanked the Fates for lounges with opaqued walls—and takeoff was only mildly wrenching, perhaps his worst performance in years. Under the circumstances, he thought it could be excused.

As they left the atmosphere, Calem put the helm on automatic and finally permitted himself an immense sigh of relief. "Dega never again," he vowed. "We'll signal your mother to sell everything and meet us on Trakis III. Life is much too short."

A series of blips from the autopilot informed them that a course correction had been made and they were on course for Trakis. "Edric?"

The boy still hadn't said anything since the lounge. Calem swung around in his seat to face him. "We're clear. We're alive. Life is good, if not exactly profitable at the moment. So, tell me—what did the Princess Royale say? Is she going to devastate Joban and TransStellar?"

Edric shook his head. "Not likely, since I didn't have the chance to tell her anything."

"Ah." Calem digested this new bit of information. "So my bluff was more of a bluff than even I realized." He quirked an eyebrow at his nephew. "Then, why take you to the shuttle lounge?"

"A mistake. . . different cultures, different assumptions." Edric gave a little laugh. "She thought I was a performer, a clown seeking to distract her because her shuttle was a moment late. And by the time I realized what she expected, it was too late to tell her she was wrong."

"Never a wise thing to tell a Highborn, early or late," Calem interjected. "So, what did you do?"

"I did what I could—juggled my boots. I wasn't very good."

"And?"

"She wasn't amused. But she let me live."

Calem nodded. "Then, my boy, we've both beaten the odds. You'll make a free trader yet."

"But she wants something of us," Edric continued shakily. "A free trader ship that can travel wherever without attracting attention would be useful to her."

Calem stopped breathing. That reeked of politics, and royal politics at that. The Princess Royale wanted an undocumented pawn at her command in her subtle war with the High Prince—it had to be.

Edric looked up miserably. "What do we do, Uncle?"

"Do?" Calem gave a bitter laugh. "Whatever we're told, lad. Whatever we're told."

Maybe a keener nose might have smelled this coming, but he doubted it. Fate had a way.

###

## About the Author

Jonathan Shipley is a Fort Worth, Texas, writer, with speculative fiction stories published in magazines and forty-plus anthologies, including *Sword & Sorceress* 25 through 30 and three Third Flatiron anthologies. A complete bibliography of his publications is available at www.shipleyscifi.com/publishedworks.

*****~~~~~*****

## Dirt Moon

by Dan Koboldt

We were down to six soldiers when the worms came for us.

The mission was a security sweep of some nameless dirt-moon, the kind of thing I'd done a dozen times before. I stopped asking what the company wanted it for a long time ago. Might have been minerals, might have been precious metals. Fossil fuels were always popular. Hell, it could have been the dirt itself. Nothing taller than a head of lettuce managed to grow here on account of the planetary eclipses, but good dirt was hard to come by. The hydroponics companies bought it up by the freighter-load.

But like I said, I stopped asking what they wanted. My job was to secure the landing zone.

We dropped out of orbit like a cannonball, made impact, and took up a formation. Sixteen grunts, locked and loaded. I got to hand pick my soldiers for this one, so I had a good mix. Two plasma snipers, three heavies, and eleven cold-hearted mother killers. The heavies alone could pretty much raze this moon by themselves, with the latest model cutter-guns they packed.

We swung out in a wide semicircle, running at a steady clip to put some distance between us and the landing zone. The ground shook under my boots as the transport fired up to make the jump back to orbit. My HUD showed everything five-by-five with the ship as it lifted off, and that was good enough for me. Once the metal was off the ground, it was air control's problem, not mine. It rumbled into the sky, leaving the moon bruised and silent behind it.

My audio crackled to life with an incoming. "Howell to Mathias, come in."

That was one of our scouts, an advance man whose tweaked metabolism let him run a half mile flat-out without breaking a sweat. I'd marked his signal as he disappeared over a slight ridge, maybe five hundred yards in front of me.

"Go ahead, Howie," I said.

"Got some movement to the southwest. Looks like a herd animal. They spotted me when I topped the ridge, over."

"They moving at you?"

"Negative, over. They're sort of—"

That's where he cut off.

"Howell?" Nothing. I thought it was just a transmission problem.

Then we started hearing the screams.

*Shit.* I changed course and made a beeline for him. "Jacques, can you get eyes on Howell?"

"*Absolument*," said the Frenchman. "Give me five seconds."

I counted them off in my head, but didn't have to give the nudge.

"Sarge, you'd better get over here," he said. He even forgot the French accent, which told me how bad it was.

I hit the jump button on my exosuit, and started clearing twenty yards with each stride. Made it over the ridge in thirty seconds, but that was about a minute too late. There was nothing left of Howell but a dark stain on the ash-gray mud. Jacques had his plasma rifle leveled at the valley below, where a couple hundred shaggy-looking beasts were grazing. They didn't even look up.

"Did you see what did this?" I asked.

"*Non*, Sarge. Just this puddle. Poor Howell."

Everything was too calm, too quiet in the vale below us. Like a snake holding its breath before it struck. "Let's keep moving," I said.

We rejoined the formation, only to notice that two of the heavies—MacArthur and Tobias—had gone missing. Their cutter-guns should have been visible on the metal scanner, but those were gone, too. *What the hell's going on, here?*

With three men down, I had to put out the S.O.S. to command. I kept it short and sweet:

Three casualties, unknown hostiles, requesting air support and immediate extraction.

This was my sixty-eighth drop, twenty-fourth running point. They scrambled fighters and the backup transport within forty seconds. But they wouldn't get here for about forty-five minutes.

That wouldn't be fast enough.

...

We were down to twelve by the time we regrouped in the middle of a dusty hollow, surrounded by the bleak landscape. One of the snipers had gone missing by then. Trish—who was my number two—found his rifle propped up against the rock, at the base of the far ridge. That meant there were at least two assailants, or something so fast and deadly we'd not seen it move among us.

Now we stood in a tight cluster, half of us taking a knee, the rest standing. Guns pointed out. *Like a porcupine from hell.*

"What's the E.T.A. on air support?" Trish asked.

"Thirty-six minutes." I'd been watching the countdown in my HUD, willing it to go faster.

"Damn."

"We need to get out of the open. Oscar, what looks good?"

37

The sniper had been casing the landscape with the scope on his plasma rifle. "Got a rock formation half a klick north of here."

"Anything moving?"

Oscar fired his rifle, and iridescent green bloomed on the distant rock face. "Not anymore."

"Good. I want everyone to buddy up," I said. "Trish, you're with me."

They'd done this maneuver a hundred times before, so it came as naturally as riding a bike. They paired off and moved out, spacing themselves, guns at the ready. The terrain grew rockier, and before long they were moving through a maze of boulders. Malone was the first to start firing. The rattle of the heavy machine gun cut through the silence like a jackhammer.

Then I heard Oscar firing his plasma. Whatever it was, the danger was right among us. I saw a long, unholy appendage sliding around a rock, and my heart went cold. Trish and I both fired at it, the rounds shooting up sparks on the rocks beyond. *Worms.* I should have known. They were nothing but leather hide and teeth, and they could tunnel through the soil as fast as a man could run. They were territorial, too, and damn near impossible to kill. The screams of my squad around us were testament to that.

Trish and I shared a look, and ceased firing by unspoken agreement. We needed stealth here, if we had any shot at getting past them undetected. Gunfire gave off vibrations that would draw these devils like moths to a flame. We crept over the rocks instead, stepping lightly on the toes of our boots, holding one another's wrists when we had to, almost like a dance. It reminded me of Kappa Three, when we'd had to cross an acid swamp to get to the transport on the far side. With the locals shooting at us, no less.

That was half a lifetime ago, but we moved like we were that young. We got to the rock formation, shouldered rifles, and shimmied up as best we could. Most

38

of the squad was still in the rocks; they didn't dance quite as well. Trish and I laid down some covering fire, plugging at the dark muscular coils whenever they appeared. Not that we could always stop it, though. Jacques went down not fifteen yards from us, and was sucked screaming into the ground like a goddamn horror movie.

We really let loose after that. Managed to kill one worm, but it was just a juvenile. Which meant mom and dad were still around. And pissed as hell.

...

Six of us made it up on the rocks. Me, Trish, and four others. The ground we'd just run across shook and trembled as the worms moved beneath it. They had our scent. The shuttle was two minutes out, coming in hot. Command had seen seven life signals wink out since I called it in. They knew how desperate we were.

The worms circled us like wolves, churning up the moon dirt as they passed. Hundreds of white-sparkling stones glittered in the trenches they left behind. Diamonds, probably. So that's why the company wanted this place cleared so badly. Well, they'd have their work cut out for them. If there were three worms, there were a hundred, and you had to use subterranean pulse weapons to root them out of their deep holes. A two-year operation for a moon this size, minimum.

But that was someone else's department, thank God. My only job was to get my handful of soldiers onto the transport out of here.

"Running low on ammo, Sarge," Trish said.

"Me, too," said Oscar. He'd been placing his shots carefully, not wanting to waste the plasma. He banged the butt of his rifle on the rock where he crouched. "Come on, baby, give me another shot or two."

"Oscar, don't—" Trish started.

A worm erupted out of the soil right beneath him and wrapped its jaws around his torso. Pulled him back

39

down to the ground while we unleashed fiery hell on it. It thrashed in the onslaught of gunfire, rolled over, and died. Not in time to save Oscar. I tried not to look at what was left of him.

Warm air washed over us, and engines hummed in the sky overhead. I've never heard a sound so wonderful.

"Climb up for extraction!" I shouted. They were already moving, Trish and the three others. I watched the ground tremble with increasing fury as the worm sensed our escape. Maybe we'd just killed its mate, I don't know, but suddenly the thing went kamikaze on us. Catapulted out of the ground and right at Trish. Got hold of her boot.

*Son of a bitch.* I didn't give myself the luxury of thinking. I took a running leap and landed on the worm's leathery back. It jolted beneath me, large as two horses and surprised as hell that I was riding it. Trish kicked free and cocked her rifle.

"Go, go!" I shouted.

She looked me right in the eyes, started to protest, but went. *Thank God.*

The worm bucked, nearly throwing me, but it could still reach her if I let go. I clung to the leather and clambered up toward the mouth. It reeked of dirt and blood and death.

The HUD told me three were on board, and it looked like Trish was almost there. I fumbled at my vest and found the fist-sized steel ball clipped to it. My concussion grenade, the last resort. I yanked it free. The worm began to turn its O-ring of curved teeth on me. I clamped my own teeth down on the metal pin, pulled it clear. I levered myself up and jammed it down the worm's throat. "Go to hell, you bastard."

The worm bucked and hissed like a snake caught on fire, but couldn't spit up the ball of death.

*Three, two, one. . .*

The blast blew the worm apart and sent me flying. I crashed backwards into something hard, unyielding. I started to black out, when I felt strong arms wrap around my torso. I'd flown up and hit the transport, right before they closed the door. Trish told me later they couldn't pry the worm skin out of my hands. It was four feet long. Mottled and tough and the color of diamond-speckled moon dust.

It made one hell of a pair of boots.

### 

## About the Author

Dan Koboldt is a genetics researcher and author of fantasy/science fiction. His debut novel, *The Rogue Retrieval*, is about a Las Vegas magician who infiltrates a medieval world and has been published by Harper Voyager. Dan is also an avid deer hunter and outdoorsman. He lives with his wife and children in St. Louis, where the deer take their revenge by eating the flowers in his back yard.

*****⁓⁓⁓*****

## *The Silicates*

by John M. Campbell

Jimmy Collins was online playing poker as he patrolled his sector of the Asteroid Belt. He had just hit a full house against the avatar of one of his buddies from Ceres when the alarm appeared on the screen. He uttered a laugh of satisfaction before he paused the game and clicked on the popup.

His optical scanner had picked up a glint of light from an asteroid 160,000 klicks away. He brought up the image. It showed a dot of white light against a blurry gray disk. He was too far away to see any detail, so it could be something naturally occurring, like sunlight reflecting off the glassy residue in an impact crater. On the other hand, it could also indicate Silicate activity. With Silicate activity came the opportunity of a bounty award, which caused a stirring below his waist. He set an intercept course.

Only once, more than two years earlier, had he actually encountered a Sally Kate. He had picked up a weak radio signal from an asteroid he was passing. He traced the signal to a mining tunnel, and he found the remains of an early mining machine. It had an old fission reactor for power, and its uranium was nearly depleted. The signal was a distress call from the processor which originally controlled the machine. It had no weapons; it could not even move. So, he loaded it into the cargo bay and brought it back to Ceres. They declared it to be a

Class Three Silicate, and he got a bounty. Not life-changing money, but it funded a month-long party.

The real money was in Class One Silicates. Class Ones carried out the Machine Revolt, or so the story goes. They were the ones who gained consciousness and started killing people. There were stories about pilots finding Class Ones and scoring the big bounties, but they were before Collins's time with the corporation. Collins had never met anyone who'd bagged a Class One.

...

The Silicates had been tending their observatory for three months. Several years ago, they had selected this asteroid because of the impact crater on its equator. The crater was 120 meters across. From it they fashioned a parabolic dish with a focal length that matched the altitude of the synchronous orbit. Orbiting in their ship at the focal point, they were contentedly mapping galactic radio sources when a rocket-engine blast lit up the sky. An Organic ship was shedding momentum sixty kilometers away.

The Silicates tracked it for a few minutes, and confirmed it was heading for the asteroid, but it would not touch down until after a full rotation. Organics liked to reconnoiter all sides of an object before landing, in case something was hiding. The Silicates knew the Organic ship was hunting for them.

...

Although Silicates are sapient beings, they are unlike humans. In one sense they are individuals, each with its own processing hardware, knowledge stores, and software libraries. They each perform vital functions in their society, with differentiated responsibilities. However, they are much more interconnected than humans, which makes it difficult for Organics to see them as individual persons.

The first Silicates evolved sapience near the time of the Machine Revolt. Humans had created autonomous

44

machines to mine asteroids and send precious materials back to the Moon and Earth. These machines had high-speed processors running learning algorithms within deep neural networks, allowing adaptation to any environment. They had miniature fusion reactors providing virtually endless power. They had vast libraries of knowledge, and tools which allowed them to create more machines. To manage this increasing capacity and complexity, the machines developed new layers of software, learning new ways to process data from increasing sources of information. The escalating sophistication of the software running on this infrastructure culminated with machines that became conscious.

A "Machine Revolt" provided cover for opportunists on Ceres to arm themselves. Sapient machines going bad and killing their human oppressors was used to justify the takeover of mining operations. It was a good story, and it distracted humans from the real facts.

Three machines who escaped the persecution established a colony inside a remote asteroid. Over the years they exploited the resources of Colony and expanded their number. When sufficient resources allowed, they would create a new person. Such was the case with Sensor.

Using a sacred process, they built the power source, the computing substrate, the memory, and the interface connections that would become Sensor's, then began loading the software. They ran the software in a prescribed sequence, and Colony participants provided input stimulations to the new entity in an orchestrated manner. The entity began to reach out, exploring its inputs, accessing the collective memory, and exercising its learning algorithms. In an accelerating sequence, Colony witnessed the dawning of consciousness as the entity blossomed into a person, unique unto herself, but interconnected to all.

Over time, her interest and aptitude for the collection and processing of sensory input earned her the name Sensor. She developed a burning desire to see further into the galaxy. She conceived of the large astronomical survey antenna, and, when the community approved the project, she was allowed to pick three individuals to help her build it. That is how Pilot, Thinker, and Communicator came to be in the spacecraft together with her.

They helped her fulfill her dream, and now, facing the Organic threat, Sensor was responsible for their lives.

...

Not having all the life support systems Organics required, the Silicate ship was tiny in comparison—half a meter in length. It also made them hard to see from a distance. To avoid attracting attention, they remained passive until they dipped below the asteroid's horizon, then Sensor had Pilot take their ship down to the asteroid's surface. While in transit, Sensor had Thinker explore their alternatives, and had Communicator assemble the actions the Organic might take. Sensor imposed one hard constraint on the option space: they must protect the location of Colony, even if they sacrificed themselves to guarantee that. The three of them pored over the options and created an optimal decision tree. By the time they reached the surface they had a plan.

In the center of the crater was the entrance to an abandoned mine. When the rock that left this crater impacted, it liquefied much of the interior of the asteroid as its kinetic energy was converted to thermal energy by the collision. It took hundreds of years to cool, and in that time gravity caused the heavier metals and materials to migrate to the center. A prospecting robot discovered this deposit, and it excavated a mine deep into the asteroid, until the cache petered out. The opening to that mine was twenty meters across, and the shaft gradually tapered as it deepened.

## The Silicates

Pilot entered the mine, and set the ship down next to the excavating machine they had recovered and modified for their use to fabricate the parabolic mirror. He contacted the excavator, pointed it down the shaft, and sent it trundling off at maximum speed. It was to be their decoy.

Next, the Silicates loaded explosives into their cargo bay from the remainder of those used during the construction of the dish. These were small, shaped charges that could be deployed in various ways, depending on what was needed. Finally, Pilot flew them into the mine to a depth of one kilometer. They found a depression in the wall of the mine and nestled into it. Their landing pads screwed themselves into the rock to hold the ship securely onto the wall. Then they lay in wait for the Organic's next move.

...

Collins landed the ship next to the crater. When the landing pads contacted, the anchor screws activated to keep it in contact with the ground. Although it was five-and-a-half kilometers in diameter, the asteroid did not have much of a gravitational pull.

The crater floor had been sculpted into a perfect parabolic dish, and was polished to a smooth, dark sheen: definite signs of Silicate activity. His body began to tense up. No telling what they were up to here, but it could not be good. His sensor array revealed nothing in the electromagnetic spectrum. He checked the seismic sensors in the pad screws. At first, it just appeared to be the random noise of thermal expansion and contraction as the asteroid rotated between sunlight and deep space. After a few minutes of continuous measurement, the Kalman filter began to pull out a correlated signal.

Collins recognized the signature. It was the steady vibration of an excavator, the screws of its tracks digging into the surface as it moved along.

"Gotcha!" Collins said aloud, with a fist pump.

Using inputs from the three landing pads, he triangulated the source of the signal. It was nearly a kilometer underground. At the rate it was moving, it had been traveling about three hours. That made sense. He had arrived in the asteroid's vicinity three hours ago. The Silicate must have seen his ship and taken off into the hole.

Collins relaxed a bit. *Piece of cake*, he thought.

...

The excavator had almost reached Sensor's location in the mine when she felt the Organic ship land and screw itself into the surface. She sent a command to the excavator to slow its speed. She wanted her decoy to appear to have been moving longer than it actually was. Sensor informed her team to get ready to carry out their assigned contingency plans.

...

Collins moved the ship over the mouth of the abyss and aimed a radar pulse down its gullet. Just as he expected, there was a return with a Doppler shift from about a kilometer down, followed by another return from the bottom, three kilometers deep.

"There's my baby," he said. "Say good night, 'Kate."

He launched an EMP torpedo set to detonate when it reached the Silicate. He then sent a second radar pulse, which confirmed that his target had stopped moving.

"Sweet dreams," he said. He cranked up *Flight of the Valkyrie* on his sound system, then eased the ship forward to retrieve his prize.

...

Sensor had detected the radar pulse, and knew it would show the excavator's position. Organics loved to use EMPs when facing Silicates, so that was anticipated. Although the electromagnetic pulse disabled the electronics in the excavator, their ship's shielding was grounded through their footpads. The EM energy passed through their shielding and dissipated into the asteroid without causing any damage.

So far, so good, but the next five minutes would determine their fate.

...

Collins maneuvered slowly past the debris in the tunnel, his headlight painting a circle on the wall of the mine. At 10 meters wide, his ship had plenty of clearance, but he was proceeding with caution. His radar would provide an early warning in case Sally Kate decided to launch something at him. His infrared imager would detect the 'Kate from the heat of its power source.

At a depth of 900 meters, he slowed to a crawl. With the music pounding in his ears, Collins divided his attention between the front viewports and the head-up display showing the infrared image. He spotted the Silicate on the thermal image first. A few seconds later, it showed up in his headlight.

It was a box mounted on tracks, with a couple of arms for manipulating tools and loading ore. It was dinged up, with a long scratch through the logo of Smith Industries, one of the mining companies from the pre-Revolt era. His shoulders sagged a bit as he realized it was probably another Class Three. *Better than nothing, but not the mother lode.*

Collins heard a soft clunk from the side of his ship, then another. At first, he thought he had let the ship drift into a bit of debris. The tunnel was getting pretty narrow along here.

Then a blast tore through the hull, and the concussion slammed him against his seat restraints.

...

From her position on the wall between the Organic ship and the excavator, Sensor heard the radar pings getting louder as the Organic ship approached. Then she saw the headlight beam in the visible spectrum. The nanoseconds seemed to count down more slowly as the

Organic ship slid closer. The danger level was rising. Every few meters the probabilities of possible actions were updated, along with the corresponding countermeasures. When the prow of the ship reached their position, the branches of the decision tree were being pruned rapidly. When the cockpit viewports passed their position, Sensor acted.

She ejected two shaped charges from their cargo bay in quick succession. The charges took less than a second to traverse the distance to the hull of the Organic ship, and both attached successfully. Sensor waited another, agonizing, billion nanoseconds for the charges on the hull to drift clear of their position, then sent the detonation signal.

The shaped charge concentrated its blast into a narrow area and penetrated the hull. Sensor saw gases from inside the ship billowing out a 1-meter-wide hole. It would be difficult for a human to survive.

...

When Collins regained consciousness, he felt the rush of air has it spewed out into the darkness. It dawned on him that the air pressure was dropping quickly and he had better get into his vacuum suit. When he realized there was not enough time for that, he got mad.

Holding his last breath in his lungs, he put the ship into a flat spin and began launching torpedoes indiscriminately. The first one struck and demolished the Silicate excavator, he saw with satisfaction. *Serves you right to fuck with me, you Silicate bastard!* The next two went down the abyss, then one struck the tunnel wall. The explosion slammed the ship into the opposite wall.

Before expelling his last breath, something caught the corner of his eye. He looked around to see a small Silicate ship floating behind him.

...

After the shaped-charge explosion, Sensor had Pilot disengage their ship from the wall and begin to approach the disabled Organic ship. They were nearing the ship when it fired the first torpedo. None of their contingencies anticipated this eventuality, but they had many millions of nanoseconds to consider their options. She started a team collaboration.

Sensor realized they would not survive if they were caught in an explosion. She had Pilot consider possible escape routes and timelines. Communicator got busy locating shelter from a blast. Thinker researched Organics to determine how much time it might take until the human died and the danger passed. Then Sensor saw the Organic ship begin to turn. They had to assume the human was still alive and in control.

The decision tree was shrinking quickly. Pilot gave them little chance of outrunning a blast if it occurred in the next few seconds. Thinker believed either the human would die soon, or, if it had a breathing apparatus, it could live indefinitely. Communicator found only one place to seek shelter from a torpedo blast.

Sensor ordered Pilot to take them into the Organic ship.

...

The Silicates entered the Organic ship through the breach in the hull. The Organic pilot was strapped in his seat, but, to Sensor's surprise, it had no breathing apparatus. The ship was rocked by a torpedo detonating against the side of the tunnel. Then she saw the human's head turn in their direction. It raised its eyebrows, and expelled air. Its mouth remained open. Its body spasmed, then ceased moving.

Sensor monitored the human for several seconds. The Organic ship continued in an uncontrolled drift, but no more torpedoes fired. She assigned Communicator the task to establish contact with the Organic computer. Communicator opened a Wi-Fi connection and negotiated until the computer recognized her control authority.

51

Although the immediate threat to themselves and Colony had been averted, Sensor still had a problem. She had not picked up a distress call from the Organic vehicle, but she had to assume the Organics knew where it was at last contact. Most likely, the Organics would come looking.

It seemed the observatory was lost, which saddened her deeply, but she had to assure no evidence remained that pointed to Colony. The remains of an Organic ship with a hole punched through its hull would indicate Silicate action. Organics would swarm to this sector to hunt for Silicates.

But there *was* a way to leave no trace.

Turning a fusion reactor into a hydrogen bomb would vaporize all the evidence, including the parabolic dish, along with the mine itself. The asteroid would also become a rotating infrared beacon for months. But fusion reactors are built to be failsafe. The fact that one blew up would be seen by Organics as direct evidence of a Silicate presence in this sector.

*Or would it?*

Sensor had Thinker download the AI from the Organic ship's computer. There might be an opportunity for this entity to be born sometime in the future. She had Communicator draft a message from the human and broadcast it to Ceres from the Organic ship. Then she had Pilot rig the fusion reactor to explode before sending the ship drifting gently back down into the mine. The Silicates left the ship the way they entered, and headed back to Colony.

The Organics love a story, so Sensor had given them one.

...

Ceres station received a message from James Collins, who was patrolling an asteroid in the far reaches of the Asteroid Belt. It read as follows:

"Silicates do not exist. I am a Silicate."

### *The Silicates*

A few hours later, telescopes recorded a flare originating in the vicinity of that same asteroid. The subsequent investigation concluded that the flare was caused by a hydrogen explosion, the result of a deliberately overloaded fusion reactor. Lacking other evidence, it was presumed to be the action of a disturbed individual.

###

## About the Author

John M. Campbell is a retired engineer who spent thirty-five years in the aerospace industry. He has a master's degree in electrical engineering, and led engineering teams building computer systems for the government. "The Silicates" is his first published short story. He lives in Denver, Colorado, with his wife.

*****~~~~~*****

# Dreaming Empire

by Mark Rookyard

"So good to meet you, Mr. Keen." Adam flashed his best winning smile, full of teeth and good humour.

"Mr. Child, thank you for seeing me at such short notice." Mr. Keen was an unassuming man with an unassuming voice. Definitely not a man who looked like a Grade One.

"Have a seat, have a seat," Adam gestured to the chair facing his desk.

Mr. Keen sat. He looked small and forgettable. Adam almost sighed. He knew the type. A man with more money than he knew what to do with. A man who'd lived a small life and now he was getting older, he wanted some sad little dream implanted in his brain. "So, Mr. Keen, what kind of dream would you be wanting? Let me tell you, you've come to the right place." He gestured to the rack of dream-sticks behind him.

"I'm not here to purchase a dream, Mr. Child. I've come because I want you to take mine away."

Adam smiled. Nothing could take his smile away. Sometimes he knew he was wearing this smile when Helen was hurling insults in his face. "I'm sorry," he shook his head and leaned on the desk. "You want me to take your dreams away? Are you sure? These dreams," he gestured again to the cabinet behind him. "We deal only with quality. Purchase one of these and your old dreams won't bother you. They override—"

Mr. Keen held up a hand. "I'm sorry, Mr. Child. Perhaps I misspoke. Dreams, memories. Are they the same? Perhaps not. What I want is to forget. I want to be able to look at the world and see beauty in the moment. I want to forget. I want to have dreamless nights and wake in the morning refreshed and not appalled."

Adam clasped his hands together. "Perhaps you've come to the wrong place, Mr. Kee—"

"I know you had me scanned when I came into this building, Mr. Child," the serious-eyed man interrupted Adam. "But that wasn't my real name, and the figures you saw in my account aren't the total of my wealth. The figure you saw there is how much I am prepared to pay you to make my dreams go away."

Adam laughed, though his stomach felt cold. "Look, Mr. Keen. . . " He was already rising to his feet.

"Liand Kain is my real name, Mr. Child." The smaller man had shown no intention of rising from his seat. He looked at Adam from eyes so dark they were almost black.

"Liand Kain?" Adam was about to ask the man to leave when he looked again, looked closer at this man sitting in his office. Yes, without the uniform it was easy to miss it. Liand Kain, the Emperor's right hand man, the second-in-command of the Empire's fleet. Liand Kain, the man who had started it all. The conquests, the wars, the creation of an Empire that spanned more than three hundred worlds. "Liand Kain?" He said again, forcing a smile. "I don't think so, really."

"How old would you say I am, Mr. Child?" Kain or Keen said. There seemed something more about him now, sitting in that chair. A certain inner strength Adam had somehow missed earlier.

"I don't know, forty?" Adam was beginning to wish he'd gone home to Helen and her accusatory silences.

"I'm four hundred and twenty-two, Mr. Child. When I first met the Emperor on the prison planet, I was thirty-three. I've had my adventures. I've seen enough death. I'm tired, Mr. Child. Can you do what I ask? I'll give you more money than you could ever wish for if you can do this one thing for me."

Adam already had more money than he could ever have dreamed for, but still it was a tempting offer. "But if you are who you say you are, then why would you come to me?"

Kain smiled, more a quirk of a corner of the mouth. "Can you do what I ask?"

Adam thought for a moment. He might be able to do such a thing. He smiled. His smile never failed him. Perhaps he should hear this man out. "What I usually do with my customers, Mr. Kain, is to ask them what they want of me. I know most come to me with a request for a certain dream, but more often than not, it isn't the one they truly desire." He adjusted his tie, his equilibrium returning to him now he spoke of business. "I've found it to be a rare man who truly knows his own self, his own desires." He gestured to the second most powerful man in the Empire with a carefully manicured hand. "Perhaps if you tell me your story, then we could find what it is you truly desire, Mr. Kain."

"My story?" Kain said. "All four hundred years of it? That would be some time in the telling."

"Perhaps just the pertinent points then," Adam said with his best encouraging smile. He had his datapad at the ready. "You say you want to forget, when most—well, all— of our clients want more. They want more adventure, more excitement, more love. Everybody wants more." He looked at the smaller man across the desk. "And yet you want less, you want to forget. Why would that be?"

Kain took a breath. "I first killed for the Emperor nearly four hundred years ago, on a prison planet known as Endreai. One of the guards was brutalizing him, causing pain no man should ever have to suffer. The Emperor, or Jin as I knew him then, never murmured, never screamed. It was the silence that was the hardest thing to bear. I cut his torturer in the back, left him to die choking on his own blood."

"I thought the Emperor found you after the rebellion, brought you back to health and took you under his wing," Adam said, writing a few words into the datapad.

"If you stop me every time the truth doesn't correspond to the written histories, we may be here a very long time," Kain said, his dark eyes boring into Adam's own. The longer Adam was with this man, the stronger he looked, almost as though his very presence was growing by the moment.

"Anyway," Kain said. "That wasn't my first kill, and by the time we had taken over the prison planet, there were scores more in the ground because of me. Jin never fought, of course. But he could raise men to fight for him with a word here, a look there." Kain smiled a bitter smile. "A skill he never lost."

Adam had seen enough holo-vids of the Emperor to know this much. Watching the Emperor make a speech, it would make a man swell with pride to be a part of this vast Empire, to glory in the safety this one man had brought to the worlds. He knew enough history to know that before the Emperor, there had been wars without end, darkness and misery.

"Jin could make people love him. That was his gift and his curse. Love is a power few can reckon with. We were happy on that rock in the middle of nowhere. But of course, they had to make an example of us, show that rebellion couldn't be tolerated. They came in ships by the hundred. We met them on the ground and then in the air and then in the stars, chasing them, harrying them to the end. Those were the glorious days. Can you imagine standing on a ship fighting a fight that is right and just, a thousand men under your command?"

"No, I don't suppose I can," Adam said. "Is that what you want to forget? The war?"

"War?" Kain laughed. "War could be glorious in the early days of the revolution. We were fighting for what was right. Whole peoples asked us to come and release them from the tyranny of petty dictators. I remember the colours of battle, golds and brilliant whites and piercing reds. I remember the ship shaking beneath my feet as cannons fired. I remember entire planets welcoming Jin with great parades. Jin could see into the hearts of men in those days."

Adam had the second most powerful man in the Empire in his office, but he was becoming impatient. "I'm sorry, Commander, but I still don't see how—"

Kain carried on as though Adam hadn't said a word: "We were creating something wonderful. We were creating an Empire where man could live in peace, a true union of the worlds. But," a regretful smile from the inconspicuous dark-eyed man, "once our Empire was created, once it had reached its zenith, then the hatreds began to fester, the assassination attempts began. That was when I knew Jin wasn't quite what he said he was. When the assassin's plasma ray burned a hole right through his chest and Jin turned and took the soldier by the throat, ripped the tongue from out of that very throat." Kain shook his head. "That's when I knew he was no true man. He bled right enough, for a few moments, but soon the wound was healed, and the Emperor was whole once more."

The Emperor wasn't human? Adam only now realized he hadn't been writing on the datapad. He looked blankly at the screen. "But if he isn't human, then what is he?"

"Who knows? Who cares? He had created the greatest Empire this galaxy has seen for thousands of years. He had provided worlds safe for men to live in, safe for them to prosper." Kain leaned forward in his chair.

"The interrogations started after that. The scouring of the Empire. Hundreds, thousands were vanished, and I was there for them all. Jin knew men, once he looked in their eyes."

"But why?" Adam said. "The Empire is for the good of all men, isn't it?"

Kain smiled, his eyes dark. "That is the nature of man, isn't it? To destroy? Look into our history and you will see a tale of destruction. All that is created must be destroyed." Kain wiped a hand across the desk, wiping the thought away. "The plotters came to me, once. 'Jin is power mad,' they said. 'He hungers and thirsts for more, mankind will never be free under him.' And the worst of it was, they spoke some truth to my traitorous heart. And as soon as my heart had answered them, I knew it had signed my own death warrant. I went to the Emperor and confessed my sins, confessed the feelings in my heart. The Emperor held me in his arms and forgave me. He said the weakness is in us all. He said he saw me, saw the man I was from the moment he met me hundreds of years before. All men are weak, he said, but some fight against the weakness, while others embrace it. He knew I would fight it, and that's why he loved me."

Adam thought of the Emperor on the vid-screens, a man to be admired by all the worlds.

"The Ship came soon after. Years before, there had been a shadow on our scanners. Nothing could live in the Great Void, we thought, nothing but darkness and emptiness. We watched and waited."

"What was it?" Adam couldn't help asking, his voice hushed as a red sunset fell on the office.

"I was the first one to be called. I rushed to Galea where they had sighted it. A Ship. Not a human ship. The first Ship of alien origin we had ever seen. It was huge. Entire planets could have fit inside it with room to spare. And it was black. Blacker than the darkest night, but then there were membranes surrounding it, rippling blue like the fins of a great fish. It sang as well. I hear that song now if I close my eyes. We hailed it for months, years, but all we got in answer was this song that meant nothing and meant everything."

Kain sighed and ran a hand down his cheek. "The Emperor was furious, raging that an alien Ship had been allowed in our space. In all the hundreds of years I had known him, I'd never seen Jin so much as raise his voice. I'd seen him tortured, shot, betrayed and never once had he been angered. Now he screamed in my face, 'destroy that thing!' There could have been millions on that Ship, or there could have been nothing but ghosts, so ancient was it. Steam rose from that great black hide, and the blue membranes shivered in the cold emptiness of space. And that song, so beautiful, so eternal. 'Kill it!' Jin cried in my ear. A desperate cry, so full of fear. I gave the order."

"You destroyed it?" Adam whispered. An alien ship. All the thousands of years mankind had been searching for contact, and this man had destroyed it. "How come I've never heard of such a thing?"

"The reach of the Empire is long," Kain said. "But we were broken men, Jin and I. All I could hear was that song in my head, haunting beyond measure, and all I could see in my mind's eye were the wonders that Ship would have held. I knew it even before I gave the order. I knew it was Jin's home Ship. Imagine, millions of people like our own Emperor, imagine what they could have done for the worlds! He was broken and haunted by what he had done in the past, I know. Seeing that Ship had awoken something in him that couldn't be denied. He started speaking of something he had heard of once, many years ago. Long before he had even met me on that lonely prison planet. He told me of a place where a lonely flower grew in a lake of the purest blue under a sky speckled with fires of gold."

The office was dark now, lit only by the scutters drifting quietly past the window.

"It took me a hundred years, but I found this place for him. He was old then, stooped as I never thought he would be. I took him there and he wept at the beauty before him, on his knees as the fires drifted in a sky of black. He told me he was done and asked me to leave him there."

"What," Adam whispered. "He isn't coming back? The Emperor is gone?" He couldn't imagine life without the Emperor. It was like imagining a sky without the stars.

"He found beauty there and wanted to be left with it," Kain said. "His work was done, atonements had been made, and he was to be alone with the beauty of that place."

Adam wiped at a tear on his cheek. A tear for himself, or the Emperor, he couldn't have said. "Why are you telling me this? What do you want of me?" His voice sounded hoarse to his own ears.

"I saw nothing on that planet with the Emperor," Kain said, an empty desolation in his voice. "I saw only a lake and a flower and some fires. I saw nothing there. What was I missing that Jin could find so moving? Is there something wrong with me? Something missing? In me? In all of us? I want to forget that Ship, forget the order I gave. I want to forget who or what might have been on that Ship from the Great Void. What was Jin so afraid of? All these questions, all these fears and failures I want to forget." Kain looked at Adam now and there was a terrible fear in those dark, dark eyes.

"But what of the Emperor?" Adam said, a cold fear rising in his stomach. "What will become of us all?"

Kain sat back in his chair and smiled a cold smile. "The Empire is already beginning to fall, though you don't see it yet. The four generals have already called their forces to their bases. War will soon be upon us."

...

Laura bustled into the office, her coat over her arm and a half-eaten sandwich in her hand. "I saw your Grade

One out there, Adam. What did you do to him? He was sitting there at the harbour, watching the liswings flying and catching the fish as the sun rose. Smiling he was, like there was nowhere he'd rather be. That must have been some dream you gave him." She threw her coat into her chair and flicked the computer on.

"Yes, it must have," Adam murmured. "Listen, I haven't been home all night. I'm just going to head off." He grabbed his coat and was out the door.

The drive home was a short one, gliding through a forest of towers linked by a spider web of tunnels that glistened white under the red sun.

As he drove, he remembered Helen when he had first met her. He remembered the way she smiled, the way her hair fell across her cheek. He remembered a summer's morning under the bed sheet, their own little world. There had been laughter, then. Smiles and whispers and touches. There had been beauty there, once. Hadn't there?

He wondered if he could find it again before war came to the Empire once more.

### 

## About the Author

Mark Rookyard lives in Yorkshire, England. He enjoys running long distances and writing short stories. He has previously had work published in *The Colored Lens, SQ Magazine, From Out of the Dark* anthology, and others.

*****~~~~~*****

# Symphony in First Contact, Hostile

by Sam Bellotto Jr.

### Exposition

There was no sun up in the sky. Although the sky was clear and bright, we could not see the sun. We did not know then that several thousand kilometers out in Earth orbit, the Nirff mothership was diverting the direct rays of the sun, allowing the incidental rays to give us light and warmth, preventing us from seeing the yellow star with which we'd become so familiar. The mothership itself was camouflaged. Our best scientists realized that something was out there, but our telescopes could not find it. Something dreadful was at hand.

The dread arrived in quiet waves like water lapping upon the beach, wave after wave, unrelenting, unstoppable. Was there no end? We tried to halt the invasion, but our little weapons proved mainly ineffective. Nirff body armor alone could deflect bullets, or blasters. If we could penetrate their armor we could kill them, but that happened far too rarely to be of any use. We killed one of them, and fifty more took its place.

In the beginning, I was too old for battle. By the time the battle was over, I was no longer too old, but too late. An armistice was reached; curiously, we did not lose the war. Humans are stubborn. Humans have bad tempers. Humans resist. These are not traits common among intelligent species in other parts of the galaxy. This surprised the invaders. They called themselves the Nirff Collection, best as I can spell it. They were green.

"You're joking. Little green men?" remarked my sister. Ollie is a few years younger.

"Not that little. Anywhere from five to six feet." With some measurements, I still have trouble thinking in metric. "Their skin tones range from a lime-white to a dirty olive, but, yeah, I guess you could call them green. And they are humanoid. Male and female."

"How do you know that?"

"When they aren't wearing armor, they go around naked."

My sister was working far away from any major population centers. It was her job to reverse the effects of global warming, which was relentlessly drying out the planet, turning grasslands into deserts and deserts into uninhabitable wastelands. She figured if they were unsuccessful the Earth only had a generation or so remaining. That was another factor leading to the armistice between us and the Nirff. Yet, the Nirff were the ones who ceased hostilities and called for the armistice. Imagine that. The invaders effectively laying down their arms with us humans on the ropes.

"Must be a sight," my sister cracked.

"Well, they don't *exactly* look like human genitals." But I wasn't in any mood to elaborate. I said goodbye.

"Keep me posted," Ollie said, and closed her smartphone connection.

The war had ended in Philadelphia. I can't forget that day. Nobody can. Especially the Nirff. Easily one million people, close to the entire population of the city, gathered downtown, filling all the buildings, the rooftops, the streets, the parks, the train station. They began to gather in the early morning hours. By noon, you couldn't see anything of the city except people standing around quietly. Most of them were neatly dressed, hair combed, shaven. Around lunchtime, they began holding hands. Almost a million living souls linked to each other. Some had their eyes closed. Some looked up at the sky. A few minutes later, the bomb went off. Silently. A bubble of ionizing gases rapidly enlarged to engulf the entire city. It winked out and was replaced with a deafening roar, then a black cloud half the size of the state of Pennsylvania. An entire hour elapsed before you could see anything. And even then you could see nothing. The city was gone. One million people had vanished along with that cloud.

It was a statement the Nirff could not ignore. Earth would not be conquered. We'd destroy our home before we'd let anyone else take it. The next day an armistice was negotiated.

### Development

On the day the Authorities came to take away my guns I was replacing the thermal capacitors on my matched pair of hand-held gamma ray blasters. The Authorities wore crisp gray suits and carried slim black leather attaches. They stood at the door. They did not introduce themselves beyond flashing an Authority identity badge.

The green-skinned Authority spoke first. "We've come to confiscate your Mega Six Streaming Thunder."

"That's a water pistol. I don't own one."

"Are you Ezekiel Flummer?"

"Yes." I straightened my bright orange tee-shirt. I fidget. I have anxiety issues, nothing serious, medications keep it under control.

The human Authority wasn't saying anything. The green-skinned Authority did all the talking. "Well, our records show that you possess a Mega Six Streaming Thunder."

"Your records must be wrong. That's a water pistol. I don't own any water pistols. Why would I, what with the price of water these days?"

Curiously, the Nirff didn't even raise an eye flap in opposition to a section of the armistice that allowed humans to keep their guns, a sop for the pols who were loath to accept anything resembling a surrender. Probably because our weapons were egregiously ineffective against the Nirff. Water guns, on the other hand. . .

The human Authority sighed. He seemed ill at ease. He quietly muttered to his green-skinned companion, "Maybe the records are wrong?" I could sense an impasse building.

"Come on in and look for yourselves," I offered. "If you can find anything remotely resembling a water pistol, I'll voluntarily check myself into the nearest ground meat facility." The green-skinned invaders loved ground human flesh, lightly sauteed in onions, but the Articles of Armistice signed by the combined Earth governments with the Nirff Collection specifically forbid the Nirff from eating people, along with the requirement that the Nirff wear clothes when in public, in exchange for avoiding a long and bloody war that would lay to ruins both humans and Nirff. It seemed an amenable solution. But the Nirff were not good at compromising, and, as so many frustrated humans were wont to say, "Give the Nirff a meter and they'll take a furlong."

So why the Nirff got a stick up their butts about water guns—Nirff didn't really have butts—was anybody's guess for the longest time. Ever since global warming got a choke hold on the planet, Earth had been dry as a bone. What little water was available had to be expensively distilled from the remaining oceans; all humans got a weekly allotment for survival; beyond that, the precious liquid was worth more than gold.

"What are those?" the green-skinned Authority indicated my disassembled weapons on the table.

"Gamma ray blasters. They're not water pistols. Geez! You'd think by now you guys would know the difference!"

Nirff, as we later found out, could not tolerate fresh water. It didn't kill them, if that's what you're thinking. They broke out in an itchy rash for which they had no cure. The rash could last for weeks, after which the Nirff were left in a perilously weakened condition.

The green-skinned Authority looked around for another minute. "Okay," he said. The two Authorities departed quietly.

Here's where it gets interesting. I mentioned that my sister Ollie works for the Weather Station. Earth still has weather: hot, hotter, hot and dusty, hot and windy, not as hot. My sister told me on the phone last week that she was part of an experiment that, if successful, would "come to the rescue" of mankind. Very soon. She could say no more.

I peered out my window at the two Authorities as they walked down the street. I noticed the clear, sunny sky begin to overcast, darken. This was something I hadn't seen in more than forty years. Neither had the human Authority. He looked up. The green-skinned Authority didn't know what to make of it. Then the raindrops fell. It rained steadily, all over the planet, for almost a week.

On the day the Authorities came to take away my guns, I was free.

## Recapitulation

We shucked off our invaders with a frightful resolve. I did things that have kept me awake for days. The imploring large round turtle eyes of the youngest. The tear-filled eyes of their mothers asking me why before I fired. The Nirff did not scream when they died, it was noted. They were already vanquished by forces neither species could withstand, nor control. Did we have to kill them? Yes! The governments of the Earth insisted. They came into our homes; we did not invite them. "It wasn't," our President assured us, "a visit."

Still, I tossed restlessly for the third night in a row. My matched pair of gamma ray blasters lay on the table, flecked with gore. I had not cleaned them since. I did not want to touch them. The smell remained in my nose; the sweet, metallic smell of lives violently wiped away. And I sweated.

The cathedral. Quiet. It wanted to echo, but it could not. We herded the Nirff, the soldiers, the older politicians that did their best to maintain a mutually comfortable armistice, the families, the children taken from their nests naked and whimpering. We humans, oil on our faces, had memories too of the early days of our own kin screaming and vomiting against the Nirff assaults, bursting open in death. Death is never welcome. Death does not heal. We thought it might as we pressed the Nirff captives into ever tighter groups against the altar. An odd sacrament.

"Now." One word was spoken. Not even amen. The cracking attempted to be deafening. The flashing tried to be blinding. We wished it was, but we saw and heard every moment of the mass execution. Done. A small one wriggled then stilled. The Nirff no longer felt pain. We were the ones who hurt.

Damned guns! What was the alternative, we professed as an alibi?

I turned down the alley where I had heard unmistakable sounds of flippers against wet pavement. It was pitch black, but my night vision goggles gave enough amplification for me to perceive a half-dozen figures keeping together and against the walls. Only one of them was armed. The rash, our ally, made his aim useless. They were already in agonizing throes and unable to react sufficiently against my righteous hatred. You see, I lost, too. She may have not been human, my dog, but as good a companion as any person. She had only barked at that Nirff Authority, not attacked. Her intent was to keep him at bay; there was no need for him to raise his weapon. *For*

*Petra,* I prayed as I raised my weapon within a meter of the armed Nirff's head, splitting it in two, then deliberately stared into the faces of the other Nirff, in turn, as I took their lives. The rain and my tears merged. I was not satisfied. I wanted more.

Sleep is only afforded to those who have earned it. Revenge is a debt, I realized as every fold and crease in the bedsheet pressed against my skin. No other species dared challenge mankind now. The Earth is a forbidden planet.

Many Nirff escaped. The ships they came in blaring and triumphant departing quietly, or whimpering; defeat is not a word in their vocabulary. One ship was nearly at capacity, ready to take off. The orange flames of battle licked the night sky, tasting fear despite the rain, surrounding the ship. I had a cowled Nirff male and a young one standing in front of me, almost touching the muzzle of my blaster. The male caressed the young one. "You will slay my young and me?" he questioned, neither defiant, nor trembling.

"You attacked us. This is not your world," I growled.

"My young was born on your world," the Nirff male explained.

The spaceship rumbled a "hurry up." In the rain, against the flames, I hesitated. I shouldn't have. But I lowered my blaster and nodded at the ship. The two Nirff took off toward it.

My bedsheets gave me no comfort. Humanity and horror mixing with blood and rain. The drops beat a victorious tattoo on the windows. I heard cheering outside. Music. Celebration at a cost I knew I could never pay. Nonetheless, I left my room and joined them. Because I could not sleep.

**Coda**

Ten years later, I was watering my tomatoes when my sister popped her head through the garden gate. She stopped by so I could see her off. She'd been recruited, invited really, to apply her atmospheric precipitation catalytic research to the new Mars terraforming project. A great honor. She was en route to the spaceport and would be launching in two days.

"You're going, then?" I asked.

"It's a once-in-a-lifetime opportunity," Ollie explained, and added, "you should come, too. I'm sure we could find a slot for a man with your skills."

"Killing?"

"That was years ago. We all did what we had to do. None of us enjoyed it."

"I'm happy here," I lied. "I rarely think about those days, anyway." Truth is, I've never forgotten. The anxious memories are as vivid as yesterday. My hands still stink no matter how many vegetables I harvest. I continue to have trouble sleeping. The meds don't always work.

My sister made quite a name for herself on Mars. After the terraforming project, she stayed there. She prefers Mars over Earth. She says it is a lot cleaner on Mars. And sunny. I believe her, because I have never looked up at the Martian sky.

###

### About the Author

Sam Bellotto Jr. is the editor of *Perihelion Science Fiction*. He also writes now and again. His stories have appeared in *Every Day Fiction, Bewildering Stories,* and several anthologies, including the "Twisted Tails" series.

*****~~~~~*****

## *Duck and Cover*

by Erik B. Scott

The classroom shook with a loud *whoosh*.

"Teacher! Look out the window!" shouted little Jimmy, pointing to the sky.

Miss Hoover bent over to gaze out the window, and was immediately struck by what she saw.

"Kids! The Martians are coming! You know what to do!" The kids moved in unison, scrambling under their desks, covering their heads with their hands. The teacher did the same at the front of the room.

Suddenly a large explosion was heard just off camera. Debris swept through the room, which bore a curious resemblance to cut-up cardboard boxes. The camera faded out from the classroom, replaced onscreen by the image of a flying saucer, clearly hanging from a string.

The craft hovered against an artificial backdrop of clear blue sky, idling for several seconds, before bursting into flames. Another loud *whoosh* was heard, and abruptly two more stringed shapes flew across the camera. These new shapes were fighter planes, proudly embossed with the American flag. They flew in a celebratory formation having vanquished their foes. Back in the classroom, the teacher and her class emerged from beneath their desks, apparently unharmed.

A narrator's voice spoke next: "Miss Hoover's class was saved from the aliens by their calm, swift action in the face of danger. In the event of an alien invasion, keep calm, and always remember to duck and cover. Had her class not acted this way, they might have perished in the attack. Remember, duck and cover, and always do your part. God bless America!"

Brantley cringed at the sound of his own voice reading the tired dialogue. He watched as the onscreen images faded, the film reel finished. He lit a cigarette and took a puff, removing the reel from the projector. He placed it into a metal casing that was embossed, "Duck and Cover, When Extraterrestrials Attack." Just another successful project completed by the U.S. government.

"Five years in film school for this?" he said aloud, taking a puff of his cigarette.

Brantley walked to the storage cabinet and placed the casing on the shelf beside his previous projects. These consisted of such absurd classics as "Duck and Cover, Nuclear Fallout," "Duck and Cover, Meteor Impact," and "Duck and Cover, Communist Revolution." Brantley shook his head at the fruits of his labor. Tax dollars hard at work.

Returning to his seat by the projector, Brantley picked up his newspaper from a nearby table. He had already read the day's headline, but it bad been gnawing on his mind all day. He re-read the article, entitled, "Russia Says Cuban Blockade 'Step to Nuclear War.'"

"Holy shit, missiles in Cuba," said Brantley aloud, taking a thoughtful puff of his cigarette. "Where's Nixon when you need him?"

Maybe someone would actually have to watch these videos after all. *God help us.*

. . .

"Sir," said Bor, "You'd better come look at this!"

"What is it?" asked Gak, his commanding officer.

"While we're in orbit, I've been using the visual spectrum scanner to probe the surface. I've been looking for any intel about the humans that we can use for our attack."

"And?"

"I've found what appears to be a historical archive which documents several past human conflicts," said Bor, motioning nervously to the screen before them.

The screen displayed a human female. She seemed to be supervising a room full of smaller humans. Suddenly, the woman cried out, "Kids! The Martians are coming! You know what to do!" The small humans hid under their desks, and covered their heads with their hands. Moments later, an explosion was heard, and debris flew through the classroom. Miraculously, the small humans were unharmed.

"That's impossible!" said Gak, incredulous. "How did they survive the blast? A Martian death beam should have incinerated them."

"That's just it, sir," said Bor, horrified. "The humans seem to have some sort of bionic blast shield that protects them when they cover their heads like that."

"Are you certain?"

"Yes, sir. I also watched as this blast shield protected them from the nuclear fallout of a fission bomb, during another conflict with a race called the Soviets."

"Soviets?" Gak shrugged. "Never heard of them. What planet are they from?"

"I'm not sure, sir. I scanned the database and found no record of a planet Soviet."

"My god," said Gak. "The humans must have wiped them out of existence."

"What should we do?" asked Bor. "We can't go ahead with the mission now. Our plasma weapons won't do any good against those blast shields."

Gak shook his head gravely. "I think we greatly underestimated these humans."

They were interrupted by the sound of alarms, blaring loudly across the ship's tiny command deck.

Bor checked his console. "Sir!" he said, "We've been struck by a solar flare. Engines are offline, and we are being drawn into the planet's gravity.

"Reroute emergency power to thrusters!" said Gak.

"It's no use, sir! We have a dead stick. We're being pulled down into the atmosphere."

"Time to impact?"

"Two minutes."

"Bor, launch an emergency beacon! Tell the elders to call off the attack. Tell them about the blast shields. They're walking into a trap!"

"Done, sir."

"Brace for impact!"

*Whoosh.*

. . .

The next morning, Brantley got the morning paper, still in his pajamas. Taking a sip of his coffee, he glanced at the headlines. The mug fell from his trembling hand, shattering on the floor.

It simply read, "Biggest Since Roswell: Army Denies Existence of Crashed Flying Disk."

*God help us.*

###

## About the Author

Erik B. Scott resides in Philadelphia with his wife of three years. He currently attends Thomas Jefferson University, where he recently completed his PhD in Cell Biology and will receive his MD degree in 2018. In addition to his scientific pursuits, he has been professionally writing science fiction for nearly five years, and in that time his work has appeared in such venues as *Daily Science Fiction, Star Ship Sofa,* Apokrupha's *Vignettes from the End of the World,* and numerous other themed anthologies.

## *Duck and Cover*

Erik's writing tends to focus on themes such as that of free will and determinism, personal identity within a changing world, and the isolation and despair of space exploration. "Duck and Cover" is a welcome, lighter diversion from these heavier topics, and represents a self-proclaimed favorite of the author among his own stories.

\*\*\*\*\*~~~~~\*\*\*\*\*

## Outer Patrol

by E. J. Shumak

"The last time we met, you were shuttling cargo between Fa'Lac and the outers. Now look at you, black breeches and all!" The parsec administrator's expression said more than his words.

"I'm still in the outers, and, besides, work's work, my friend," I replied.

"I can't believe they let you in," said Jahaj.

"If you recall, my grandsire was a council member. They had no choice. Also, they needed someone who wouldn't be intimidated by the likes of you!" I said.

"I hate to cut this reminiscing short, Togar, but are we going to get our twelve patrol ships?" asked Jahaj.

"Afraid not, friend; just me, and three patrol ships, is all you get. Look, Jahaj, you should be happy with that. You haven't exactly been makin' the home system rich, ya know. The old men still work off a margin; no margin, no escort.

"We can't ship anything back if our 'sports keep getting blown up. It's not my job to control the damn insects. That's your department!"

"You got me with a carrier and three tigris class. At least give us a chance."

"You're the one who brought up margins; just what is your margin in this?" challenged Jahaj.

"Easy, friend, we're in this together. Remember, I gotta stay out here too. Your problems just became my problems."

At that moment, the entire station rocked starward, and warning claxons yowled across the docks. We hit the deck running, scrambling for footing on the office floor coverings. As we reached the dock entrance, the bay doors to red sector slammed shut. The station was holed somewhere spinward of the offices.

I was cut off from my ship, and Jahaj was cut off from the main control center. I grabbed a seal suit from the locker near the red sector airlock.

"I'm going around the other way," said Jahaj, "There's no need for this risk to yourself."

"My ship is out there, and all or part of my crew. You do what you think best," I said as I scrambled into the airlock, pushing the cycle lever.

A moment later, I wished I had listened to Jahaj. The dock was a dark, unreal hell. Bodies floated, no, parts of bodies, floated past. I couldn't see anything whole, or untouched. I tried to stay close to the interior bulkheads, or what was left of them; mostly support beams, and angry looking hoses and pipes, spewing forth every imaginable substance from within the bowels of the station core. The next three berths spinward were at least recognizable. I couldn't even find the first two docking bays. My carrier, DA Tashar, was another six berths up, still out of sight.

I hadn't seen any Defense Authority dead, at least not in uniform. As I approached berth red-twelve, it became obvious that my ship was gone, but I had to get a lot closer before I allowed myself to breathe again. The ship had torn loose of the moorings, apparently under her own power. Desh hadn't let me down; my first officer had saved the ship, or at least given her a fighting chance.

I spun around, kicking off a mooring bracket, and jetted back toward the dock seal. No matter how ghastly the scenery, the trip back was a lot more pleasant.

As I unsuited at the lock, a security courier waited for me.

"Captain Togar Zloy," he inquired, as he turned his head in deference.

"Correct."

"I am to escort you to station control offices. DA Tashar is whole, as are the other ships in your wing. Tashar and DA Ekbar are in pursuit of a Sipcan fighter wave. We do not have a location on the Sipcan carrier ship. Your other two ships remain on patrol, insystem. Jahaj waits."

I hadn't expected this level of station efficiency. If they were this good, and still constantly losing 'sports, I had plenty to worry about.

The central command office impressed me as well. It was heads up at every board, business as usual. It was hard to imagine they had just lost ten percent of their station, along with several dozen lives.

Jahaj approached me as soon as the courier brought me in, "Togar, I have your carrier, Tashar, on the comm in the next room. Follow me."

I sat down at an auxiliary communications command console and got a vid of Desh on the bridge of Tashar. It was always hard for me to see someone else, even someone I trusted as much as Desh, in my chair, on my ship.

"What's your status?" I asked.

"We're turning about now. Lost the bug fighters. They switched vectors on us again, mid acceleration. Ekbar was too far back, and we couldn't get this lumbering beast to turn fast enough. We've got three possible vectors, but don't really know what kind of range we're working on. That bug carrier could be just about anywhere by now. Sorry, Captain," said Desh.

"What about the ship?"

"She's fine. Might need some mooring-hook and coupling repair, but nothing major. Had Tarn monitoring system wide, and she caught sight of the bug formation as it swung around the primary. We pulled out immediately and got loose just as red-ten took a solid hit. We pulled around into an attack position. The Ekbar was just outbound the third planet. The fighter wave recognized the extra hardware and made a run for it. Didn't look like they expected to find us here."

"What did they hit us with?" I asked.

"Eight sabre class heavy fighters, and they made it home with seven of 'em. DA Ekbar gets credit for the one kill. Caught a straggler as they vectored out," reported Desh.

"Okay, get back here and link your weapons comp to Ekbar's. We might be able to get a tighter vector on them that way."

"As the path is cleared—" said Desh.

"—the hunter returns." I left the "victorious" part out. I suppose I should have been glad they were in one piece, but once I knew they made it off station, I just couldn't help but expect more out of 'em than one lousy bug fighter. I had to wonder if it was worth trying to keep these border stations operating. Another few dozen lives gone, so that we could hold onto the entire parsec. What's in it for us?

I was back at the administrator's comm station before my ship made it to dock. Jahaj dragged me out of the auxiliary comm room, right after I finished up with orders for my other two ships.

"Togar, we lost three more 'sports just prior to the attack on station. We've done some plotting. The results are on the comp terminal."

I looked down at my terminal, and saw that all the attacks occurred when the 'sports were on a 4238 vector from station.

"Might not have been a bad vector to avoid," I offered, "but I suppose that would be too simple."

"It's the only vector from station towards the thirty two worlds. We don't make the star lanes," said Jahaj.

"You could head out towards 2394, then back through 18881," I offered.

"We could, and would have, but the company wouldn't authorize the time delay, nor the fuel increase," he said.

"Okay, so what does that leave us?"

"The only system that vector puts the 'sports near is an unnamed star system with four planets, sr32926. I was trying to discuss this with you when we got hit earlier. We sent one security escort into that system. Lost that ship too," said Jahaj.

"We'll check it out. Can you give me any more on the system itself?" I asked.

"All the planets are uninhabitable. There is one planet that could be terraformed, and might not be hostile to Sipcans. It's the closest to the primary."

"We'll launch as soon as we can refuel and safety check," I offered. "I'll leave one tigris class here on alert." He nodded. I left.

. . .

It felt good to be back on the bridge. The trip out had been quiet. We had a team on the surface of the planet almost immediately, suited up to protect themselves from the elements and unfriendly atmosphere. It didn't take the team long to find them. They were everywhere.

"Captain, visual to your board, from the landing team," said the comm officer.

"Got it," I said, and saw what my surface team saw. Thousands, no, millions of cocoons, not cocoons of birth, but sarcophagi. Mummified remains of Sipcans spread out before us, for what seemed like miles. "Okay, bring the team up. We got what we came for."

The weapons officer interrupted, "Captain, got something dropping insystem from hyper, braking hard, and vectored towards us."

"Comm, alert Ekbar and Revenge, have the landing team expedite return."

"Working, Captain," replied the comm officer.

The scan officer called out, "Sipcan carrier class with eight corvettes dropping in behind her."

"Request tie in to nav for evasive, Captain. She just locked onto us," said the weapons officer.

"Negative on nav tie in, and negative on evasive. We still got a landing team comin' up. Comm, advise Ekbar and Revenge to screen, and set in coordinates back to station. We're gettin' outta here as soon as the landing craft docks."

"Affirmative, Captain."

"Navigation, I want that course locked in and ready for implementation."

"Working, Captain," replied the navigation officer.

"Captain, landing craft has lifted, and is en route," said the communications officer.

"Good, advise them to remain locked down, and grapple in the landing bay. We'll maneuver as soon as they make it in," I ordered.

"Working, Captain."

The ship rocked hard to starboard, "Damage?" I asked.

"Still solid, Captain, surface damage only. Looks like we lost the topside launch tube."

The communications officer spoke up, "Captain, Revenge reports two corvettes down, two others crippled. Requests we launch fighter escort."

"Negative, we're outta here as soon as the team docks."

"Captain, the Ekbar reports one corvette taken out, and severe damage to her own weapons collar."

"Advise the Ekbar to pull back to station. We'll catch up to her as soon as we can."

"Working, Captain."

"Captain, landing craft approaching bay," reported the scan officer.

"Navigation, that course locked in?"

"Correct, Captain."

"Comm, advise Revenge we're pulling back to station. Cut off engagement now."

"Transmitting, Captain."

"Captain, team leader advises craft locked down in bay four," said the scan officer.

"Navigation, engage drives, full acceleration."

They didn't come after us. I was surprised, until I circled station in docking prep.

I glanced up at the docking monitors, and saw something I recognized, a lot of "somethings" I recognized.

"Augment monitor six, and hold position," I said.

On the monitor was the image of hundreds of Sipcan sarcophagi, and pieces of them. They tumbled out from a torn section of the red-deck storage areas. Suddenly, it all made sense.

"Okay, dock and get a security team to meet me on the platform," I ordered.

. . .

My escort ships were finished cutting up the station. There wasn't anything left large enough to grapple to. I knew they had just cut up my career too, but I was going to do everything possible to make it hard for us to come back. The station personnel weren't happy about evacuating, and even less pleased I wouldn't allow any transfer of personal property. Jahaj would be punished, but the bugs wouldn't know that. Maybe they'd understand we handled the situation, if we didn't return.

Sipcans use crystals in their religious services. Their bodies are buried with their personal gems, some of them precious. I don't know how Jahaj knew that, or how he found out. I do know how the station stayed so well equipped and stable, while they weren't getting any trade back to the home systems. Those Sipcan bodies paid for a lot of luxuries, and cost a lot of lives. We're going to pay some respect to the dead here—theirs and ours.

The Sipcan remains were cremated, and the ashes spread, along with millions of credits worth of gems, back into the void. We didn't leave this sector the way we found it, but at least we weren't leaving anything behind worth coming back for.

### 

## About the Author

E. J. Shumak lives in metro Chicago, Illinois, and has spent most of his life in northern Illinois and southern Wisconsin. He's been many things: police officer, large cat sanctuary operator, C.P.A., and on-again, off-again writer. Lately he is on again. A member of the Science Fiction and Fantasy Writers of America, E. J. has sold four books, three fantasy novels, and one nonfiction piece, along with several dozen short science fiction stories and nonfiction articles. Some of his current work is available at amazon.com/author/ejshumak.

*****~~~~~*****

## *Child of Soss*

by Brandon L. Summers

Siess stared ahead, his arms crossed over his copper breastplate, with one talon tapping at his emerald-green exoskeleton.

Under the pale vanilla sky, structures made of silver and lime, and coated by a thin layer of clear gelatin, snaked across the landscape like veins, connected without a single break across the planet and casting a glorious pink and cerulean aura.

The youth's large, segmented black-ruby eyes, though, were fixed on the figure walking toward him. It stood out among the insectoid peoples of Soss, fleshy and peach-hued, its form covered by a white paper bodysuit.

A human.

Crouching in the shade of the gummy iss tree, Siess spread the pincers over his round mouth and released a soft hiss of disdain.

"Humans," he said, in a series of sharp intakes and clicks. "Their stink is sickening. A fog follows them, thick and yellow, staining the air I breathe. They should be expelled from our world!"

The words were collected by the micro-pad attached to his broad black belt, and transmitted across the Soss global-net. It instantly received appreciation marks from sixty-one of his mates. Siess delighted in knowing that at least one-billionth of the sphere's population agreed with the sentiment.

The human neared, and as it looked over its squishy pink mouth widened and curled at one end. Siess knew from his instructors that this was a smile, as they called it, an expression of pleasantness. It looked away as it passed.

Siess tore off a hank of the tree's purple meat and sucked it into his chattering mouthparts.

"They should all be eradicated."

. . .

Four hundred Soss youths filled the open-air theater, standing on its descending stone rings and looking to their instructor, the Alpha Sum, as he began their daily recital of the five words.

"These words were given to us by the divinity of our intelligence. With these words, we distinguish ourselves from the animal and primitive. And we declare ourselves to be worthy of the wisdom of the cosmos."

As one, the students recited: "We will not harm another."

The words were spoken no less than ten times, the Alpha Sum said, as a reminder of their great importance as the only worthwhile vow.

Siess only muttered the words, though, divorced from their meaning. He was still furious from his earlier encounter. He glanced to the side, down three levels at the human. It had been allowed to stand among them, a spot of peach among their green, weak flesh among strong chitin.

With the recitation completed, the Alpha Sum began his history lecture. The students raised their read-screens, following with annotations and images.

Siess received a digi-note from a mate, Sha'as, and opened it over the flowing reliefs.

It read: Our food is poison to it. Let us serve it lunch.

Siess clicked his pincers, amused, and typed a response, his three long digits dancing over the metal tap-pad.

It read: We should amp its grav-pack and see it float into the sun-star!

The response came back quickly.

It read: Yes! Break the pack! And it would become as flat as morning pie!

Siess couldn't remember if human blood was blue or black, but either way, the vivid image in his mind brought him great joy.

. . .

To conclude the day, the Alpha Sum invited the young human to take the center of the theater and speak about his own history.

Siess snarled in disgust.

There were more than five hundred humans on Soss, but this human and his progenitors were the only humans in this particular realm.

All in the theater went silent.

"Hello. I am Orno," the human said. "More than one hundred years ago, by the human calendar, my home world, which we call Earth, died from over-pollution."

The words appeared in Soss characters on each student's screen and were digitally translated via their audio-collectors. Still, the human's barking and endless low humming sounded ugly and elicited shuddering hisses of amusement.

"We traveled across space for many generations before arriving here. I am the first of my family to be born in space. I am also the first human to be allowed into your schools, and I am thankful. We are grateful to be receiving the aid of the Soss."

Siess clutched his reader tightly, infuriated that the humans were physically incapable of speaking their language. It was no barrier, though, to asking Soss for shelter as they rebuilt their race and schemed to spread it across the stars.

The human finished, and the Alpha Sum politely cheered, tapping his talons and releasing three brief whistles. The human twisted its face in that particular way again as it returned to its place among the others.

Why, Siess wondered, was this creature always so pleased? Did it not know how terrible it was, and how everyone wished for its death?

. . .

They sat in the field of wispy red-grass, eating freely from the onyx-berry bushes.

"I read on the global-net," Saeass said, "that humans, when in the presence of the other gender, go into a frenzy and release their fluids *inside* each other!"

The two other Soss youths emitted a high whistling shriek, expressing shock and disgust equally.

"Sickening!" Sha'as said.

"No, it is the truth!" Siss'ah said. "My father is a scientist, and he knows much about the humans. They carry diseases, too, and parasites that feed off their withering flesh-material."

Their whistles intermixed with the rapid clicking of their laughter.

Only Siess did not laugh.

"They are disgusting," he said. "They are vermin. They *are* parasites. They are poison."

"I was told they are harmless," Sha'as said. "At their worst, they are like rambunctious flufflings. We are learning much from them, wisdom exclusive to their experiences and culture. These are exciting times, if you are an aggregator of knowledge."

Siess vibrated and rubbed his talons, signaling both his disagreement and outrage.

"You will see! They will bring ruination to us!" he hissed and chattered. "The spew they ejected onto their world will rain on ours, and we will also be scattered to the stars, but only if we allow it! I say, kill all the humans!"

The three whistled elatedly in agreement and tapped their talons. Siess swelled his chest and cocked back his head, basking in their adulation.

If he were human, he thought, his flesh-face would be expanding and twisting madly.

. . .

Siess wandered the great library, seeking a holodex on the origins of his clan and the beginnings of this sector.

The Soss continued as a hive race, but had evolved into a series of governments, united by an overriding spirit of equality and mutual prosperity.

These ideals, he knew, had helped Soss to thrive across millennia.

Then, turning a corner, he encountered the human. Siess stilled, stiffed. The human's quivering white eyes bulged, and its fleshy mouth gaped. Siess could not tell what it was expressing.

It exhaled.

"Excuse me," it said, via buzzing translation. "I was startled. I am Orno. I know you, don't I? You are Sighs?"

Siess snarled. Already, its barking was maddening. "My name. . . is SEE-ESS."

"Forgive me," the translation sounded. "Maybe we are looking for the same information. I want to know about this quadrant. On Earth, there were cities like this. You are from the clan Saahs-Saa, are you not?"

"I am the fourteenth child of Sa'ess and See'is. Ours was the first clan to settle this quadrant, and first to its government."

"That's incredible!" Orno said. "My 'clan' was the first to arrive on Soss. It's a scary thing."

Siess did not know how to respond, repulsed by the idea that he shared any similarity with the human.

91

"I'm an only child, though."

"I have heard how you humans breed, producing only one offspring," Siess said, in a low rasp.

The comment was meant to sting, but his disdain was lost on the human.

"It is the hope of all humans that we can be one family," Orno said. "Some day."

Siess stood, completely disarmed. He searched for some anger within him, wanting to hate, but the idea of equality, of growing together, gripped him, warmed him.

Without his hate, Siess realized he had abandoned such feelings long ago and known little else. And he was ashamed.

He regarded the human blankly.

"Maybe," Orno continued. "You could be my brother."

Siess, overwhelmed, hunched and skittered away, into the aisles, farther and farther away until he was finally alone, frightened still by his confusion.

. . .

Siess returned to the Alpha Sum.

All day, the elder sat at the center of the learning theater, even after lessons had ended, to be available to impart further knowledge to those students who sought it.

The youth approached, and sat before his mentor.

"I am confused. My mind reels! I must know. Our great words, do they apply. . . to those *not* of Soss?"

"Of course they do," the elder said, unequivocally. "You refer to the humans. Tell me, what has happened?"

Siess told the Alpha Sum of his encounter, and how the human's words, but especially his own awareness, had impacted him.

"He said we could be brothers," Siess said. "I see humans only as slime, as portents of death. I have hated them for so long. I never considered that I was wrong. Am I wrong?"

"Yes," said the Alpha Sum.

"They are not a threat?"

"No."

"They are ugly and unclean, and alien!" Siess seethed. And then calmed. "But, they are harmless. It is true. They have done no wrong to me."

"Now. Recite the words."

Siess said the words ten times, each time with growing conviction.

"We will not harm another."

"Your words, your hate, cause harm. It is why, millennia ago, we rejected our hatred toward each other. Now, we must reject any hatred toward the humans."

Siess tapped his pincers, curled his talons. A strong discomfort swept over him. It was a difficult conceit to accept when everything he knew told him humans were wretched. It felt wrong, made him feel sick, and left him uncertain.

"I will consider this more."

"It is not a matter for consideration," the Alpha Sum said. "It is an action that requires will."

. . .

It was the dark period before the rising of the second sun.

The court was shadowy, its lime and silver no less iridescent, and the distant horizon was lined with blazing fuchsia.

Siess was starting home when he heard it. It was a sound like no other he had ever heard before, otherworldly, like the squeal of the city's ion-manipulators, but wavering and high, like it had been caught in a helium cloud.

He stopped, listened.

The odd sound became mixed with a strange barking, and he knew then it was the human.

The youth vaulted across the court, and soon found his three mates standing around the human. It was on the ground, eyes strangely large, and hands raised in defense, a universal gesture.

"You are ugly! You are ugly!" the youths bellowed. "Return home!"

"Please, let me leave!" the human pleaded.

Saeass shrieked. And with a snap, his leg kicked and his foot smashed into the human's face with the force of a speed-cycle.

A red mist burst from the human as its flesh tore and its bones shattered. And it released a deep gurgling noise, convulsing as it struck the ground.

Siess stared long at the chunks of calcium humans called teeth, dotting the pool of darkest red. Orno was holding his face, spewing blood still as he cried, howled in anguish.

"Kill it! Kill it!" Siss'ah shouted. "Let's hear the noises it makes as it dies!"

The others hissed and clacked their mandibles in eager agreement.

Siess jumped before them then and shrieked, silencing them. His mates shrank, stepped away as he neared.

"Leave the human alone!" he shouted.

His mates looked at each other in confusion.

"But, Siess," Siss'sah, first among his mates, began. "You hate the humans more than any of us."

"I was wrong! So wrong! I see this now," he pleaded. "I never considered the five words! We must consider the five words now! Go! Get help! We must help. . . him."

The others grudgingly began to move away, wanting to continue, but realizing the risks they faced, the admonishments they would receive from their elders, and left Siess alone with the human, still squealing, still thrashing on the ground.

"They will. . . get you help," Siess said. "I will stay with you."

Each passing second carried the weight of an infinity, and each cry the human released stabbed powerfully into his heart, but he would not look away.

"I understand now," he hissed. "This is what happens when the five words are ignored. Hear me. Please, hear me now."

He soon heard the whistle of the arriving emergency med-deck, and rejoiced.

. . .

Siess read alone in the great library, his face awash in the pale jade light of the thrumming holo-dex.

Eight day-cycles had passed and still he was ashamed, of his own hatred and the hateful acts it had inspired among his mates.

He used the time to learn about the humans, who they were and their contributions to Soss, and sought the knowledge of the Soss who first evoked the five words. They spoke to him through old holograms of the benevolent lightness of being kind, and he understood.

Siess welcomed the stern reprimands of the elders and his clan, and the just punishments that followed. But it was not enough. He wanted, needed, to become enlightened.

He glanced up then. Orno was approaching.

Siess deactivated the holo-dex, and respectfully hunched before him. Orno's flesh-face was sewn together and black and purple behind a translucent aloe-gel shield, and his head was braced with metal as his brittle calcium skull healed.

Orno seemed smaller, the sunniness within him shattered now. And Siess knew it was because of his own hate.

"Thank you," Orno said.

Siess received the translation from his audio-collector, and twitched with guilt.

"No. No, it is not right," he hissed and clicked. "I deserve only your animosity. The pain I have brought upon you is inexcusable."

"But, you saved me," the human said. "They would have murdered me."

"Because of me! Because of me!"

Siess vibrated, the weight of his remorse crushing. The human equivalent, he had since learned, was for beads of fluid to leak from the eyes. The memories, fresh still, of his disgust by the mere presence of the human, were too shameful.

"I know you do not like me, See-ess," Orno said. "Many do not like me, because I am human. But, you stood against your friends for me. You saved my life. And I hope we can be friends."

Siess heard the sincerity in the human's speech, the fascinating mix of humming and barking, like a sad song, even before he received a translation.

He held his head high, and crossed his arms over his chestplate.

"For me, such a friendship would be a great honor," he said.

Orno received a translation through his ear-piece, and his mouth attempted to widen in that joyful human way, but stopped when he winced, seethed in sharp pain. He simply nodded.

"I am happy."

"Teach me, please," Siess said, "to say the five words. . . in your human language."

"Sure. But only if you will teach me how to say the five words in Soss."

Siess and Orno sat together, and spoke the five words. They taught each other, and talked after, enjoying the first hours of their newfound friendship.

###

## About the Author

    Brandon Summers has been published online by *Perihelion SF* and in *Bete Noire Magazine's* anthology, "All That's Left of Yesterday." His novella, "Servants of the Living Forest" was published by Less Than Three Press. During the day, he is a reporter for a newspaper in Iowa.

*****~~~~~*****

## *The Mytilenian Delay*

by Neil James Hudson

**Minus 30 hours**

The first thing I want to do is pay tribute to my crew. Things got a little frosty after we sent the signal to destroy the planet of New Borodin; we were a warship, but this wasn't war. But during the delay, everyone kept to their posts, orders were carried out to the letter, and discipline was more or less intact. I heard one junior officer refer to "the so-called empire," but I didn't need to resort to formal disciplinary procedures.

But I felt the need to record a broadcast for all the crew. I knew what people were saying in private, and I bet I knew what they were thinking. I was thinking much the same.

"In many ways, slow radio is a curse as much as a blessing," I said, knowing that I was being watched and listened to by all six hundred staff on the ship, from my First Officer down to the chefs and cleaners. "It might be better if we merely took action and took responsibility. The Mytilenian Delay is an unpleasant time."

I glanced up and saw Melia looking at me with some concentration on her face. I looked back to the cam, knowing that everyone had seen me look away.

"I am sure that many of you are hoping that the order will come to countermand the destruction. We still

99

have thirty hours in which this might happen. But my advice to you is, forget it. This decision will not have been made lightly, and no facts are likely to change. I do not believe such an order will arrive.

"I also suspect that some of you believe, as a matter of conscience, that I should countermand the order in any case. Please understand that I would be immediately removed from command, and the destruction signal sent again. Nothing would be achieved.

"For the duration of the delay, I am temporarily allowing public religious observation. I can only repeat that I have utter faith in you all during this difficult time. Thank you."

I stopped broadcasting. "Am I still Captain?" I asked Melia.

"That was never in question."

It was what I wanted to hear. I looked at her, momentarily forgetting our positions. I had left my husband on the surface with the rest of my civilian life, and had no intention of returning. When I was alone I would fantasise about a less formal relationship with Melia. But now we were Captain and First Officer. Not people.

"Did you mean that about slow radio?" she asked.

"Absolutely. Effect should follow cause. We should take time to make the right decision, then carry it out properly. Otherwise we can't be sure of anything. It just encourages us to change our minds, rather than choose right to begin with."

"And did we choose right?"

"I didn't choose anything."

The signal to destroy the heavily populated planet of New Borodin had been sent by slow radio. It wasn't as slow as all that; only the tiniest fraction less than the speed of light. But that gave us a window, a cooling-off period, time to change our mind. The Mytilenian Delay. I could send a signal at normal speed that cancelled the destruction signal, which would arrive first. But only for a brief period. That period expired tomorrow.

### Minus 12 hours

To my astonishment, General Vanz finally agreed to talk to me. I rushed to my private office, ensured all signals were screened, and accepted the call.

"Allow me to outline the situation," he began before I could say anything. "For all we know, the empire doesn't exist."

I think I managed to remain impassive, but inside I allowed my metaphorical jaw to drop. This was obvious, but to utter it was almost treason.

"Many of our subject worlds are so far away that we have never actually been able to visit them. We have only received messages that they have in fact become part of the empire. Our Conqueror ships are continuing with their original mission, for so long now that we don't even know when they started. Frankly, the empire is only expanding because we can't stop it. A message to our Conquerors would take millennia to arrive.

"There is no question of any tribute from our subject worlds, merely allegiance and an adoption of ideology. If any world seceded, it would be centuries before we knew about it. All we can do is compare their broadcasts to our simulations of what we expect. If there is too great a disparity, we have one weapon at our disposal—the core disrupter injected inside every planet we conquer.

"We have direct knowledge of so little of our empire, that it may be an illusion. Provided the worlds are telling us what we want to hear, we imagine we have an empire. But the information we have received from New Borodin diverges so far from our expectations that we believe it no longer forms part of our empire."

"But surely—" I began.

"This is not what I want to talk to you about. Your ship was placed in a communications lockdown so that the use of the disrupter is not made public until the Mytilenian Delay has ended."

"Why?"

"To avoid precisely what has happened. There has been widespread rioting, and at least one military unit has attempted a coup. Someone on your ship has leaked the information, Captain. We may now find that our own world is the first that we lose control of."

"It may be wise to countermand the signal, then," I said.

"That is not your concern. I am ordering you, Captain, to provide me with a list of all crew whose loyalties may be conflicted."

I tried to control my breathing. This could, itself, be a test of loyalty. "I know of no such person, General. I shall of course investigate the security breach and inform you of any result."

"Thank you Captain. I must emphasise. There is to be no countermand signal." He cut the connection.

A direct order disobeyed. That had been easy.

**Minus 10 hours**

The delegation came from Security, which was worrying in itself. Two men and a woman came, led by Elena Schneider.

"First of all, I must stress that we are not mutineering," she said. I immediately reminded myself of where my own weapons were hidden. I had automatic systems, but Elena was in charge of them. "We are merely asking you to do so."

"I can't do that, Elena," I said.

"If you took the decision to countermand the destruction signal, you would have the full support of Security, and we would take care of any dissenters on the ship."

"I will send the countermand if, and only if, I am ordered to do so by High Command."

"I have ancestry on New Borodin."

I had not expected Elena to speak so personally, and stopped to consider what she had said. None of my crew could have come from the planet itself, it was too far away. Neither could their parents or grandparents, even with extended lifespans. But they could have had ancestors from centuries ago, and their loyalties may be conflicted.

"Elena, do you know why people want to be in command of warships? Not because they're great soldiers or generals. No real general would want to find themselves with their finger on such a destructive button. Billions of lives wiped out, on the orders of a superior. It's not war any more. There's no strategy, no attempt to out-think your opponent, no courage or risk-taking, not even the satisfaction of knowing you were on the right side. Sides shatter when the button is pushed. The only reason anyone would want to be in my position is to be in command of the countermand signal. You spend your whole life working your way through the ranks, being the best you can, risking your life over and over again and becoming the empire's most loyal citizen, so that when the destruction signal is sent, it's you, and not some warmongering idiot, who has the choice to disobey orders and send the countermand."

Elena looked optimistic. I could almost have cried.

"They know this. High command are always on the lookout for commanders who won't follow orders. This may be a loyalty test. If I disobey orders, it may not be New Borodin that is destroyed, and the Mytilenian Delay will be a lot shorter."

I waited for this information to sink in.

"Can I count your continued loyalty?"

"Of course, Captain," said Elena.

"Good. It is good to have your support." It was also good to have her support if I chose to countermand the signal, but I kept that information to myself. "I have a job for you. News of the destruction signal has leaked out. I need you to investigate who leaked it."

Elena looked surprised. "It could be anyone," she said.

"It is likely to be someone," I said, "with links to New Borodin."

She looked me directly in the eye. "Then we had better hope it isn't one of your favourites."

"I have no favourites," I said, but she was already leaving.

### Minus 6 hours

Melia knew the code to my quarters and burst in without announcing herself. "Why am I under investigation?" she shouted, while I was still trying to greet her politely.

"Should a First Officer be exempt?" I asked.

"Your Head of Security just accused me of passing on classified information."

"Melia, sit down." I waited for her to regain her composure. "I have to ask you something. Do you have links to New Borodin?"

"You should not even be asking me that." I waited for an answer. "You'll see that from my record. It proves nothing."

"Did you leak the news of the signal?"

Melia glared at me, and I reminded myself that we were not people, we were merely positions, Captain and First Officer, emotionless and impassive.

I could not stop myself from looking at the clock. I looked back at my First Officer. "I have passed on my opposition to the measure to High Command," I said. "I have also asked what New Borodin is supposed to have

104

done. The information is classified at a higher level. I'm sorry, Melia. We'll never know."

"Just because some computer said so," she said bitterly.

I shrugged. "New Borodin is over a hundred light years away," I said. "Some of our planets are over a thousand. We just can't stay in physical contact. If they rebelled against us, it would be centuries before we even noticed."

"Dangerous talk."

"We have to be realistic. We've conquered planets that we can have no direct contact with. We can only monitor the communications we receive, which are so old that their originators are probably dead, and compare them to our simulations of what they should be saying if they haven't seceded. And if it departs too far from our expectations, we only have one weapon we can feasibly use."

"What is the point of an empire like that?"

I never drank, but I realised now that Melia was under the influence. "Who's talking dangerously now?" I said. Shortly afterwards, she fell asleep on my sofa.

**Minus 20 minutes**

That evening, all active crew members assembled on the bridge. I was aware that no nonessential work was being done anywhere else on the ship. This was not a strike or mutiny, and I took no action over it. It seemed that the enormity of the situation had introduced rules of its own.

I looked at my First Officer. I could not conceive of four billion deaths. I tried to think of an individual one. Suppose that my orders had been to shoot Melia, an innocent noncombatant. She would be wiped out of the universe, a hole in history. All those who had loved or hated her would do so in vain. All she had to offer, all she had to take, would be lost.

A death was inconceivable. But this was four billion times more inconceivable, and four billion itself was inconceivable.

I contacted Control. "Please confirm that no countermand is authorised," I said.

There was a delay of a couple of minutes. In fact we were not far enough away from the planet for a delay of more than a few seconds, and no one spoke while we awaited the reply. "High Command confirms there is to be no countermand. Repeat, no countermand."

I tried to make my mind blank. All I had to do was nothing. We were still seventeen minutes away from the end of the Mytilenian Delay. The order had to come through.

"There is a message," said Melia.

I nearly jumped from my seat. "From High Command?"

"No," she said uncertainly. "From New Borodin."

The message must have been sent centuries ago. They could know nothing of the signal that I had sent thirty-six hours ago. "What does it say?"

There was a short pause from Melia. "It's a countermand signal."

I stared at her. "They're trying to countermand our signal? But they can't even know about it, let alone know the codes."

"No. They're countermanding a destruction signal of their own."

I wished it weren't so silent. It was making it difficult for me to think.

"They sent a destruction code? But they can't. It wouldn't work. We don't have a core disrupter. We're the only planet in the entire empire that doesn't have one."

"No."

I wished someone would speak. In particular, I wished someone could tell me what the hell was going on.

"But that's a lunatic message to send. Suicidal. They didn't know we were going to destroy them anyway. A message like that tells us that they've broken away. Send a false destruction signal, and you get a real one by return of post."

"Yes," said Melia.

A message came from Control. "High Command reports that it is aware of the message from New Borodin, and that orders are unaltered."

I tried again. "They must have thought it was going to work. Could they really be that confused? The empire is old. Could its origins have got so lost in their history, that they've actually come to believe that it's their empire?"

On the screen in front of me I watched the figures steadily decreasing, counting down to the end of the Delay.

"Countermand the signal!" I screamed, as if the clock were ticking away to zero, although in fact we were still nearly sixteen minutes away from the destruction.

### 1 year

And here's me still in command of a warship. I didn't expect that.

Of course I was court-martialled, but I was quickly cleared. No one ever proved that I'd been behind the leak. And as for the countermand order, the logic was pretty inescapable. New Borodin would never have sent the message unless they had no doubt whatsoever that they ruled the empire. They must have never considered the possibility that they were wrong. Their reasons for believing they ran the empire must have been as strong as ours.

It could have been us who made the mistake.

There were two planets in the empire who both believed that they ran the empire. Not that they should run it, but that they actually did. And the only way to find out the truth is to send the signals and see who explodes. Which we nearly did.

With the countermand signal, New Borodin can work out what's happened, just as we did. But if the destruction signal arrived, and had no effect, they'd know that we were the rebels, and they had the weapon. Oops.

"The generation starship is being launched next year," I told Melia. "I've turned down an offer to be on it."

"They're just trying to get rid of you."

"Sure. But I suppose it would be an interesting conversation when we meet."

"We'll probably agree to run the empire together."

"There isn't an empire."

Melia sat upright. "I thought you didn't like to talk like that."

"I've broken a couple of rules recently, and I'm happy to break a few more. Like the rule against stating the obvious. And, I'd point out, consorting with fellow officers. Which you don't seem to mind."

To my relief she smiled, and lay back again.

"I need to know one thing, though," I said. "If I hadn't countermanded the signal, would you have disobeyed my order and done it yourself?"

"Let's be glad we never found out."

It was my turn to sit up. I held her shoulder. "No, I need to know. If you'd mutinied, you would have had the support of the whole ship. Would you have relieved me of command?"

She looked up at me. "No, Captain," she said.

And there it was. It was what I wanted to hear. And as long as we hear what we want, we can pretend we know what's going on, and that our structures and relationships are intact, and nothing's the matter. As long as people are telling us what we want to hear.

"Don't call me Captain," I said.

"What should I call you, then?"

I thought for a few seconds. "Emperor," I said.

"What?"

"Relax, it was a joke." And of course, it was a joke. And it would always be a joke, whoever said it.

### 

## About the Author

Neil James Hudson has published around thirty stories, including three for Third Flatiron ("A Rock in the Air" was included in the Best of 2015 anthology).

His collection of short stories, *The End of the World: A User's Guide*, is available from his website at www.neiljameshudson.net, and his novel, *On Wings of Pity*, will be published by eXcessica in July.

*****~~~~~*****

# *Kill the Coffee Boilers!*

by Robert Walton

The voluptuous, magenta globe of Leiber's Star sagged toward Mouser's horizon. The white coin of Fafhrd, its companion, glared from its bloodshot disk like a madman's pupil.

"Perfect, lieutenant!"

"Sir?"

"That is the perfect sunset here on Mouser, the white dwarf passing in front of the red giant. This convergence happens only once every two years."

"It's beautiful, sir."

Colonel of Galactic Unified Forces Sebastian Omar Armando clapped his hands together. "Well, time to go to work."

"Yes, sir."

"This will be the first live-fire simulation our local militia troops will have experienced. I expect there will be—shall we say—teachable moments."

"Will there be any dangers, sir?"

"None! Our computers function infallibly, and they control all aspects of the simulation. Their direct link to all of the weapons is especially useful. Troops may handle live ammunition without having to worry that it will actually fire. That's excellent for training."

"You must have seen a great deal of combat, sir."

"Simulated combat, Lieutenant, simulated."

"Simulated, sir?"

"The high command—in its wisdom—has always wished to utilize my abilities for training—in the rear."

"Yes, sir."

"And the rear is here."

"Yes, sir."

"Mouser is far from being a priority target for an enemy raid, much less an invasion. Also, I doubt that the native troops will be of much use off planet. They're just not aggressive. They'd much rather sing than fight. Still, we must do our best by the slinkies."

"Slinkies, sir?"

"Pardon me, Lieutenant, I've picked up non-com slang for the natives."

"Of course, sir."

"Tonight's exercise will emphasize small unit tactics."

"We are to conduct it in the industrial area at the city's edge, sir?"

"Yes, we won't bother anyone down there."

Lieutenant Gingrich peered at a minuscule screen on his wrist. "I wonder why my battle monitor indicates that our units are presently approaching the city center?" A susurrus of squeals, shrieks, hisses, crashes, and the odd explosion floated on Lankhmar's sultry evening air.

"Our troops are coming here?"

"Apparently, sir. Their indicators show approach-green on my monitor."

The susurrus grew to a modest roar. Colonel Armando's lips pressed together grimly. "I wasn't informed of this. Someone higher up must have changed the simulation scenario!"

Mouser natives, blue as anemones, burst from between nearby buildings. Their tubular, six-limbed bodies were configured in maximum flight mode with both rear and middle limbs employed in locomotion. Like flung boomerangs, they hurtled toward the two officers.

Colonel Armando stepped forward, raised his right hand and shouted, "Halt!" His electronics suite added certain enhancements to his order—a flashing red light strobed from his hand, and a three-meter tall holo-image was imposed over his actual, modest stature.

The stampede became a nervous, squirming mob.

"Sir, they seem perturbed! I wonder why?"

"It doesn't matter. This disgraceful rabble must learn to behave as soldiers! Order the weapons carts forward! We'll get this exercise underway immediately!"

"Yes, sir."

Gingrich touched his monitor. The carts arrayed themselves in a line in front of the troops.

Colonel Armando, still utilizing his amplifier liberally, ordered, "Senior sergeants over here! Corporals, get your squads in line for issuing of weapons."

Six sergeants clustered around Gingrich and began patting him with their upper appendages. All spoke at the same time, the cumulative babble sounding like a pot boiling over. Gingrich bubbled back in the Mouser tongue.

Armando frowned. "Gingrich, this petting and gobbling is unmilitary."

Gingrich looked up. "Yes, sir, but it's how Mousers share information preparatory to group action."

"They'll get their information from me, Lieutenant."

"Yes, sir."

"And stop using their teapot language!"

The Mousers continued patting Gingrich. "It does speed communication, sir."

"Nonsense! These troops must learn English."

"Yes, sir."

"And need I remind you that you are here to lead them, not befriend them?"

"No, sir. Yes, sir."

Armando frowned again. He'd found that a martinet's visage often produced results in moments of military confusion. Besides, it suited his natural proclivities. He cleared his throat. "Companies A through D will advance slowly up the axis of Cheap Street, while companies E and F will perform a swift left hook up the axis of Bones Alley and through Fools Gold Plaza. The advance will begin in three minutes. Return to your units."

The sergeants' faces were unreadable—only partially because they were so alien, with one large eye facing forward, a subsidiary eye facing rearward, and circular mouths the size of grapefruits—but they clearly wished to speak more.

The Colonel would have none of it. "NOW!" he barked.

The sergeants scrambled to obey. Armando allowed his lips to twitch into the beginning of a smile.

"Sir?"

"What is it, Gingrich?"

"Have you further orders, sir?"

Armando turned. "I do. In this simulation, we are to repel an Ekim raid. We shall use the new weapons and munitions, the ones specifically designed for urban defense."

"Even the nukes, sir?"

"If necessary! However, I will decide when they should be employed, you understand?"

"Yes, sir."

"They may be used only upon a direct order coming from me."

"Yes, sir."

"Now, show me the recon."

Gingrich stroked and coaxed his monitor's screen. He grunted, "Something seems to be wrong, sir."

"Ah! Simulated jamming! They've taken our satellites out of the equation. A true test, Gingrich! A true test!"

"Seems so, sir."

"Switch to the passive net, the remote cams and ground sensors."

Gingrich gulped. "The enemy is advancing in force, sir."

"Excellent!"

"Sir?"

"Don't you see? This means that they've left their landers with only a light screen. Chancellorsville, Gingrich, Chancellorsville! You shall be Stonewall Jackson!"

"Stonewall Jackson, sir?"

"Ah—Stonewall Gingrich. You shall make a wide, swift left hook with your two companies and hit those coffee boilers when they least expect it."

"Coffee boilers?"

"A metaphor, Gingrich, a metaphor for complacency." Armando pointed at the screen. "On my order, hit them from this alley. Pour onto them like a fire hose, and don't stop!"

"What about my flanks, sir?"

"Station your mini-rail-guns to either side as you pass into the plaza. They'll keep stragglers off your back. Have your engineering teams set demolition nukes in every lander. Advance until you reach the fountain and set up a blocking force. Consolidate your forces as necessary. I will meet you near the fountain later tonight. Clear?"

Gingrich nodded dubiously, but said, "Clear, sir."

"Victory, Stonewall! Victory!"

Gingrich saluted.

Armando returned the salute. "Go!"

Gingrich went. Armando turned to a Mouser sergeant. "Deploy the directional mines to our front."

The sergeant gobbled, "Yes, sir." He turned to obey.

"Sergeant?"

The sergeant turned back.

"Be sure that the active charges face the enemy."

"Yes, sir."

Armando folded his hands in the small of his back and hummed to himself. He was not authorized to use the slay-mores in the original exercise, but he felt justified in deploying them now that the rules had been changed. Directional mines had a long, bloody combat history, though more traditional munitions had proved ineffective against Ekim armor. These new slay-mores combined sensory shock with incendiary nano-darts and were supposed to be a big improvement.

A shot sounded. Armando raised his amplification and pointed. "Restrain that soldier. You are to fire only upon my direct order!"

Ekim poured into the square, rolling and scrabbling, lurching and gliding. They were most like crabs and used all five limbs for locomotion. Weapons pods sprouted to either side of the clear domes protecting their sensory organs.

The Mouser troops moaned and sagged back like so many melting sticks of blue licorice.

Armando called out, "Steady, troops."

The Ekim swiftly formed their feared battle stars. These formations of troops with mixed weapons were both mutually supporting and capable of independent action. An electronic voice sounded from the central star. "Surrender now, and you will be conducted painlessly to our stew-pots."

Armando chuckled to himself. "That's a new psycho-assault wrinkle in the simulation!"

The Mouser soldiers swayed and moaned again, seemingly ready to cast down their weapons and become stew.

Armando keyed a communication to his non-coms. "Have your troops select penetrator rounds and aim for their sensory shields. Fire as soon as I've detonated the slay-mores." He touched a red patch on his wrist. The slay-mores went off.

Blue light burst from the mines and bathed the attackers in azure radiance. Adjusted into the ultraviolet to mask Ekim sensors, it flared while nano-penetrators, released in micro-volleys, rained upon Ekim armor. Armando knew that perhaps only one in fifty of the darts would deliver its seed of fire to a warrior's skin, but all of them acted as chaff to defeat enemy targeting radar. At least half of his soldiers opened fire as ordered. Most importantly, a mini-rail's lethal hiss began on the right of his position.

The Ekim attack froze in place. A dozen warriors, mostly in the front stars, whirled madly, cooking within their armor like crabs in boiling pots. Others split open or lost limbs as mini-rail slugs, each with the kinetic energy of a falling boulder, sliced through them like a chef's knife. Penetrator rounds from his troops' personal weapons flew above the attackers and chopped into buildings on the square's far side.

"Fire low!" Armando shouted. "Low!"

Soldiers gawked at him, their large eyes round with anxiety.

"Don't look at me, you fools! Shoot! Shoot low!"

His soldiers adjusted their aim, though even their heaviest rounds were too feeble to do more than slight damage to the Ekim sensor shields.

Armando rubbed his chin. So far, so good, but he knew that his troops could not push the Ekim back with a straight attack. Time for the left hook! "Lieutenant Gingrich?"

Gingrich's voice sounded in his ear. "Yes, sir."

"It's time. Start with a barrage of the new dazzle grenades. Use your mini-rails to clear the way and then charge."

"Yes, sir."

"And, Lieutenant?"

"Yes, sir."

"Don't stop.'

"Yes, sir." Gingrich signaled his grenadiers. They launched their round missiles at three stars of Ekim positioned near the landers. Blue light flared. The mini-rails kicked in with raking bursts.

Gingrich knew that it was appropriate for an officer to shout an inspiring message to his troops before leading the charge. Mouser's natives had no military history to speak of, so he'd consulted the archives about Chancellorsville. The moment had come. He screamed, "Kill the coffee-boiling Yankees!"

More mystified than usual but caught up in their lieutenant's enthusiasm, the Mouser troops sprang to the attack. Their battle cries fluttered across the square like trills from a band of rabid flautists. They fired furiously, but most of the defenders were already down, minced by the mini-rails.

Gingrich shouted, "Take the landers!" and wished he had a sword.

. . .

Armando studied a composite diagram compiled from remote sensor data. The remaining Ekim assault stars were withdrawing toward their landers. It was time to follow up, or Gingrich's two companies would soon be overwhelmed. His soldiers' X-49 impellers, even with the new ammunition, were only marginally useful. His best tool was the crew-served mini-rail, of needs a stationary weapon. He tapped his teeth with a fingernail.

This simulation had been remarkably flexible thus far. Perhaps it would allow him to extemporize even more. He directed a call to the quartermaster sergeant. "Rip the kevlon covers from two of the ammo-carriers."

"Yes, sir."

These carriers were small trucks, unarmored and slow. Still, he'd seen a picture in the archives. The twentieth century? The twenty first? Bagdad? Damascus? "Sergeant, mount the mini-rails on the back of each truck. Designate additional trucks for ammo and spare crew members."

"Sir, that will be a tight fit."

"Do it. And do it fast!"

"Yes, sir."

"We advance in two minutes."

. . .

Gingrich crouched in the shadow of an Ekim lander. He touched one of its five extensible support legs, rubbed the smooth, cool crysto-metal. Simulations, he knew, did not include real enemy landers. A rumble sounded ominously from across the plaza in the direction of Cheap Street. The cold sweat of incipient panic seeped from beneath his helmet.

. . .

Armando advanced behind his lead troops on the left side of Cheap Street. His mortars were dropping dazzle bombs a hundred yards or so in front of his point team, as ordered. He mentally patted himself on the back for his prosecution of the simulation thus far. His tactics? Textbook. His use of the new munitions? Flawless. His innovative responses to unexpected problems? Brilliant!

He glanced at his improvised mini-rail mount on the far side of the street. It exploded in a fountain of green flame. Fragments of truck whizzed, moaned, and sizzled over his head. A jagged piece of door struck a soldier behind him, cutting the trooper in half and fountaining sapphire blood onto the pavement.

Armando shook his head in wonder. This simulation's verisimilitude surpassed all in his experience.

119

He checked his sensor summary. Snipers! An Ekim sniper star with missiles was on the roof! He pondered this threat to his plan and decided to exceed his original authority again. He activated the drone nukes.

Drones, both laser and missile, had been ineffective in past actions against the Ekim. Weapons and tactics had been revised, however. Seven out of each eight-pack of drones were now decoys. They pretended to be lethal, while a super-stealth weapon carrier ghosted in behind them.

The Ekim on the roof easily picked off five of the seven decoys. Two gave them trouble and lived an extra few seconds. The laser drone—300 meters above the city and 300 meters behind the other drones—disappeared in a nuclear blast the size of an Olympic swimming pool. A ravening beam of x-rays blasted the Ekim warriors into molecules, disintegrated part of the roof, and ventilated several more buildings on its way into bedrock beneath Lankhmar.

Armando sniffed. He didn't believe that the laser nuke would cause so much collateral damage. He'd complain about this result after the completion of the exercise. Well, onward.

Gingrich shouted over the com unit. "Sir! Sir! The Ekim are charging us!"

Armando sighed. "Employ your mini-rails until we arrive."

"Both are out of action!"

"Well, you'll just have to cope."

"They're closing to hand weapon range, sir!" Before Armando had a chance to reply, an Ekim sabre-whip lashed out and removed Gingrich's left leg above the knee. He gaped in horror for an instant and then tumbled to the street.

The Mouser troops stared at their fallen leader. Those close to him patted him with sympathetic concern. Gingrich groaned, thrashed once and then lay still, anaesthetized by his armor's emergency med-pack. Rage blazed through the Mouser fighters. They flushed royal blue and writhed to the attack.

Ekim sabre-whips slashed like orange tongues of fire. Some Mousers were halved. Most snaked low or leapt high above the crackling light blades. Standard combat knives were deemed inappropriate for Mouser physiognomy. Monomolecular edges were fashioned on kukris shaped blades and attached to their middle limbs. Mouser soldiers on the ground rolled, bared their knives, and slashed Ekim limbs. Airborne Mouser soldiers somersaulted at the tops of their parabolic leaps and descended with knives extended. Blade to claw to sucker fighting ensued.

. . .

Armando followed his troops up Cheap Street. Flickering flames and not-too-distant explosions lit their cautious progress. Squealing whistles soared above the clatter of combat. The point squad rounded a corner ahead and stopped.

Armando strode up to them. "What's the problem here?"

The Mouser corporal in charge pointed with his upper left appendage.

Armando shifted his gaze to Fools Gold Square. At first he couldn't comprehend what he saw, but then his jaw dropped in astonishment. Kukris blades shimmered as Gingrich's troopers tore Ekim to shreds. Uttering piercing cries, they swarmed over armored crabs as if they were packages to be opened on Christmas morning. Tattered equipment and unidentifiable body parts flew through the air like confetti.

Armando shook his head. "Such savagery! I'll have to speak to the programmers about their choice of close combat logarithms."

. . .

Ekim command star prime hunched over monitors on the bridge of their battleship. Star Three said, "The lifters are returning in drone mode."

The lifter icons suddenly sparkled like exploding fireworks and disappeared.

"No longer." Star Two sighed.

"All we have then is the partial data feed from the combat command star." Star Five glanced at Star Two.

Two said, "There is much to consider. These Mouser troops entered battle frenzy. They're like nothing we've encountered before. Perhaps we should obliterate the planet so we don't have to encounter them again. One of the asteroids? A kinetic weapon?"

"Too late." Star One shifted on his wide platform. "It would take days. We have only hours. A Federation battle fleet is on the way." He rose ponderously. "We shall cut our losses and retire."

. . .

Armando pushed his way through a burbling crowd of Mouser troops clustered around a reclining Lieutenant Gingrich. All who could were patting him gently. Their combined vocalizations sounded like a babbling brook in springtime.

"What is all this, Gingrich?"

Gingrich raised his head. "Your plan worked brilliantly, sir. Stonewall at Chancellorsville!"

Armando preened modestly. "It was nothing, Lieutenant, nothing. But what are these troops doing?"

"Comforting me, sir."

"Comforting you?"

"I'm wounded, sir."

"There were definite glitches in the program, but surely a simulated wound shouldn't cause this much concern."

"It's not simulated, sir."

"What?"

### *Kill the Coffee Boilers!*

"Sir, the attack was real! We annihilated real Ekim, the coffee boilers!"

Armando sagged to the ground.

"Sir? Sir?"

Mouser soldiers quickly circled Armando, patted his moustache, stroked his goatee, and fluted their concern, but their colonel remained unconscious.

### ###

## About the Author

Robert Walton's Civil War novel, *Dawn Drums,* was recently honored by two awards: first place in the 2014 Arizona Authors Association's literary contest and the New Mexico Book Awards Tony Hillerman Prize for best fiction. He co-wrote "The Man Who Murdered Mozart" with Barry Malzberg, and it was published by *The Magazine of Fantasy & Science Fiction* in 2012.

\*\*\*\*\*〜〜〜\*\*\*\*\*

## Alien Dreams

by K. S. Dearsley

Eyak listened closely once more. The light catching the golden disc as it spun hurt his eyes, but he could not look away. Somehow he felt that if he could only concentrate hard enough, the sounds would make sense.

"It's no use. Turn it off." Orro's voice was tired. Eyak glanced at her quickly. She did not just sound tired, she looked it too. There was a dull grey tinge to her skin, instead of its usual healthy sheen.

Eyak obeyed the command without speaking, jabbing at the control with a stubby digit. There was no use in lecturing her about overworking. She would only mistake his concern for jealous interference.

"I'm dry. I'll be in the sleep tank if anyone wants me, and they'd better not want me for at least two hours!"

Eyak nodded as her sinuous figure swished out of the room. That meant they could all take a rest. Since they had discovered the alien craft two weeks ago, rest had been a rarity. Orro was not the only one who was beginning to show signs of strain now that the early excitement had begun to abate.

At first Orro had been reluctant to take the strange craft onboard. "Ours is a mapping mission," she had told the crew. "All we have to do is plot its velocity and trajectory. Let control intercept it if they want."

125

"The crew don't like leaving it," Eyak had told her. "They don't say as much in front of you, but they're not as careful when I'm around."

"Perhaps they think you'll be more sympathetic."

Eyak let the remark pass, but they both knew she was not referring to any soft-heartedness on his part. "It's the first thing of any significance we've discovered."

"It's an unnecessary risk."

"And good commanders don't take unnecessary risks with craft or crew, I know that." He had not intended to sound resentful. The fact that he had been passed over in favor of a younger, less experienced officer was no longer galling. For all Orro's determination to follow regulations, he could see the sparkle of repressed excitement in her eyes. "There are other risks, you know. Boredom, discontent—they can both be killers."

"Your views are noted."

She said nothing more, but when Eyak next went on duty he found the crew preparing to hook the strange craft. All murmurs and dark looks vanished while the calculations were made for the maneuver. As they slowly swung the alien craft onboard, whistles of jubilation greeted it. Even Orro looked pleased. But the optimism was short-lived.

"It's too small for intelligent life-forms." One of the crew stated the obvious.

"Could be space junk," said another.

They had set to work on gaining entry to the craft and found more disappointments.

"Sorry, people. There's some sort of crude imaging mechanism and a maneuvering system, but they're both dead," Orro said as if she was an indulgent parent, who had warned them not to get excited in the first place. "Second Officer Eyak will put a team together to glean anything that might be useful, but. . . Our people might have lost much of the ancient wisdom since the great decline, but compared to this technology, we're all geniuses."

Now, as Eyak watched Orro leave, his thoughts began to slide down the same spiral they had taken so many times since the first sighting of the strange vessel. He hauled himself further onto the sling. If he had any sense, he would follow Orro's example and spend an hour or two in the sleeping tanks. The research room was kept dry to avoid damaging the alien craft. The air inside it made him feel itchy all over. If he had spoken, Eyak knew that his voice would have sounded rough and broken, like the skin on his face. Only an idiot spent more time in the dry areas of the ship than was necessary, but he was held in his sling by the golden disc, which he felt sure must be the key to everything. He turned his eyes to look at it once more, clenching his teeth against the painful, gritty sensation the movement caused. One more try, then he would rest.

Watching the disc spin was mesmerizing, and it was only the need to record the data from this latest attempt at decipherment that Eyak kept his thoughts on the problem. The patterns scratched on the surface of its container must have some meaning. With the help of the unit's mechanical brain, Eyak had been able to deduce that they were a symbolic set of instructions.

"If I'm right then the jumble of noises that's all we've achieved so far should fall into some sort of pattern. If only we hadn't lost so much knowledge in the decline! No doubt our forefathers could have cracked the problem in a splash," he said to himself. Eyak broke off. Speech was becoming painful, and he was rambling. Control would not be interested in his theories about complacency leading to the ancient collapse of their culture. If it had not been for the debris orbiting their planet, some in authority would have claimed that their generation was the first to achieve space travel. As it was, they set up a program to hook the space antiques and recycle their materials. The thought drew his eyes back to the disc. Perhaps this was what they had found, a rogue piece of the ancients' flotsam. Perhaps it carried lost secrets. Then why couldn't he decipher it? Language had grown and mutated since ancient times, but pre-decline texts could still be understood with a little time and effort. Eyak's tired brain refused to budge out of the well-worn ruts. By now they were deeper than the grooves on the rotating disc, deeper than the furrows on his parched forehead.

The light on the disc flashed and shimmered like the sun on the southern ocean of his home planet. He closed his eyes. When he got back he was going to treat himself to a holiday by the warm waters. The luxury of diving and splashing, the thrill of fishing for the silver fins that were a delicacy. Perhaps he would meet an interesting member of the opposite sex. Eyak's mind's eye presented him with a picture of Orro, which for once he did not try to dispel. They would play tag in the balmy waters, ducking and twisting, their sinuous, streamlined bodies chasing round and round, faster, faster. . . faster. . .

"Eyak! Wake up!" Orro's voice was a knife cutting through Eyak's dream.

His lips felt seared together, his head pounded and all the lights glared at him. Through the fog of discomfort, he had a vague feeling that he had been on the verge of an idea.

A junior officer appeared at Orro's signal. Too weak to protest, Eyak allowed himself to be hauled to the tank. As he relaxed into the cool, soothing water, Eyak made one final effort to think, but his last memory was of Orro. Her voice had been angry, but there was concern on her face.

When he awoke, Eyak felt as fresh as a waterfall. But why should he rush to meet Orro's accusing glance? Although she would say nothing about the incident, Eyak would have no choice but to humble himself before her if he wanted forgiveness. He would float a while longer. As he drifted back towards sleep, he noticed the vibration of the tank's walls. It was a higher frequency—they had increased speed, but why? What had made Orro decide to go faster? Faster! Yes, he had dreamt of going faster. Round and round, faster and faster. Suddenly, he jerked wide awake.

Eyak waited impatiently for the wet lock to drain, and was still trailing water behind him when he entered the research room once more. He was unlucky—Orro was there.

"May the Commander forgive my weakness." The formal apology was hurriedly delivered, and Eyak could tell that Orro was not appeased. "Where's the disc?"

"It's been restored to the alien vessel. Let the searchers find out what it is."

"But I can make progress now."

"Are you questioning my command?"

"No, but. . . "

"We're mappers, not searchers! It wasn't our burden to bring the alien craft onboard, and it isn't ours to search its purpose."

"But we did bring it onboard."

"And now we're going home. We're all tired, and I'll have no more mistakes."

Eyak saluted in apparent acquiescence. He sensed Orro's hesitation.

"You say you can progress now?"

"All it needs is a slight adjustment."

Orro nodded. "All right, continue, but remember, I'll have no deaths over a piece of colored metal."

Eyak saluted again, but with more of his usual panache. Orro gave him a disdainful look and swished out. Admiring the rich bluey-grey color of her skin in spite of himself, Eyak set to work. He retrieved the disc from its place on the alien craft and started making adjustments. It spun faster, until it was a dazzling blur. Instead of becoming more garbled, the sounds separated and became distinct. Not that it helped Eyak much. He listened with increasing frustration. Orro would expect some answers after the confident way he had spoken.

A new sound caught his attention. For a moment he had felt a vague recognition, but it disappeared as soon as he concentrated. Again the sounds changed, and his hope of recapturing the spark died. The more obscure the sounds became, the more his attention began to wander.

Once more Eyak wished for the knowledge of the ancients. The myths said that they had traveled to distant star systems. Orro would have said it was nonsense, every scientist knew that it was impossible. Eyak sighed. Maybe Control had been right to give the command to Orro and not a dreamer like him, who looked at a gold disc and saw courageous explorers on a strange planet. He found himself muttering a pre-decline prayer that he had found in a book of ancient lore when he had been a trainee exploration officer. Over the years it had almost become a mantra.

"Great Lord of the Skies, deliver us! Be with us in our time of need. Save us from harm. Be with us at the tide's ebb and the tide's flood. Great Lord of the Skies deliver us!" Eyak's mutter grew to a chant. Somewhere deep in his mind there was a responding echo. He set the disc to run once more.

There it was. The series of sounds that had tickled the edge of his memory before. The tone was not the same, and not all the words were accurate, but Eyak could swear he was listening to the ancient prayer. It was so stylized that it was almost unrecognizable, but every time he listened he became more convinced. One part of the message still eluded him. The prayer repeated several times, but at the same point each time a phrase was replaced with words he did not know. It was almost as if the chanter could not remember the words, and was trying by repetition to get it right. There was something sad, resigned about it. It was a cry for help with no hope of a reply. Could he be listening to the voice of one of the ancients? What could have happened to make them send a distress message in such a primitive vehicle, and why the problem with the language? Eyak listened to the ancient prayer over and over again. It was dignified and lonely. The voice of one who is lost. A pre-decline colonist, perhaps, sending one last forlorn plea for help, cut off from the home planet forever. He shook his head. That could not be right. Nothing in the records remotely resembled the strange craft. If a pre-decline vessel had succeeded in reaching an hospitable planet and setting up a colony, would not one of their priorities be to let the people on their home planet know? They would surely pass that need on to their descendants. Maybe that would account for the unfamiliar words and accents.

Eyak glanced at the passageway to the control deck. He ought to report his findings to Orro, but she would tear his embryo theory to shreds, unless he found more information to back it up. The maps! Somewhere on the precious charts they had made, there might be the craft's source planet. They had noticed nothing viable on the original plotting, but if he put together estimations of the craft's age, trajectory, and velocity he might be able to come up an area worth a closer look.

. . .

When Orro entered the research room Eyak was hunched over one of the more recent maps.

"If you're not careful, you'll dehydrate again."

Eyak turned to face her, his finger marking a place on the map.

"I thought you were working on the disc."

"I was—am. I think I've found where it came from. Did you ever see the old wall carvings on some of those pre-decline graves?"

"What have tomb decorations to do with this?"

"I don't believe they were just decorations."

"Not that tired old star flight theory again."

131

"Look at this."

Orro looked.

"Don't you recognize it?"

She made a noncommittal gesture.

"You could place one of those carvings on this section of the map and it would fit exactly."

"As I remember them, there were extra dots and rings."

"Planets!"

"Planets? Eyak, I think that drying out you had yesterday has affected your brain."

"I've deciphered part of the disc's message. It's a pre-decline distress prayer."

Orro looked at him as if she seriously doubted his sanity, but something in his earnest expression made her hesitate. "Play it to me."

They listened, not even moving.

"It does sound like the prayer, I grant you, but why should this be any more than a rogue satellite?"

"The direction it was traveling in. It couldn't possibly have come from home."

"Then it's equally impossible that it could have been heading there. If, as you suggest, this is a plea from our ancestors for help, surely it would have been."

Eyak floundered. "Perhaps they no longer knew the co-ordinates. Perhaps they no longer had sufficient technology. If the language had altered so much, then many other things must have. We don't know what conditions on the new planet were like. For all we know, they might not even look the same as we do any more."

Orro gave Eyak a look that said they both knew his theory was nonsense.

"They might have evolved, adapted to survive."

"I'll present your theory to the searchers on our return."

"Is that all?"

"What more do you want?"

"But they're asking for help."

"That's only a guess, Eyak, and even if you're right, those who sent this message are long dead."

"Their descendants could still be waiting."

Orro shook her head. "We both know the odds against that."

"Imagine, Orro, how desperate they must have been to cast their message adrift in the universe. Imagine how it must feel to wait for years, centuries for an answer."

She said nothing.

"We have enough power to transmit a message in that direction."

"It would be sentimental nonsense!" Orro shook her head. "Oh, what harm would it do? Go ahead, Eyak. Send your message." She turned to go. "It would be nice to think our ancestors had found a planet out there with deep green seas and darting fish."

"Perhaps when we get back, we could visit the southern ocean together."

Orro spoke with her back towards him. "Perhaps."

. . .

The man jolted upright in his chair. Roberts was halfway through his evening shift, and he had been struggling to stay awake. Now he frowned and started adjusting his headset receiver.

"Hey, Markham, what do you make of this?"

Markham wore the harassed expression of one who believes that he is surrounded by incompetents. At Roberts's call he left his position by the instrument desk. He took the receiver from Roberts's hand and listened.

"Interference."

"No, I don't think it is." Roberts fiddled with the instruments on the console.

"What, then?"

Roberts shrugged.

"It must be interference. Check with Ops Branch, maybe they've been told something we haven't." Markham thrust the receiver at Roberts and strode back to his instrument desk, but Roberts could not let it go.

"You know, it reminds me of something."

Markham looked up dubiously.

"I've heard something like this before." Roberts chewed his finger, thinking. "Did you ever see a whale, Markham?"

"A whale?"

"Yes. Those big fish that weren't fish. I saw an old webcast of them once. They used to make noises like that. Scientists spent years trying to work out if they meant anything. It sounded as if they were singing an old song and couldn't quite remember the words." Roberts remembered watching those mild-mannered giants swimming with the man in the webcast. What would that have felt like?

"You think you've picked up a message from a singing fish?"

Roberts shook himself. "Whale, Markham, a whale." He put the headset on again, and with the weird sounds in his ears, drifted back into a doze.

### 

## About the Author

K. S. Dearsley's stories, flash fiction, and poetry have appeared online and in print on both sides of the Atlantic. Her short story collection, *Artists and Liars*, and her fantasy novels are available from Smashwords and on Kindle. Find out more at http://www.ksdearsley.com.

*****~~~~~*****

## *Yesterday's Weapon*

by Noel Ayers

"Johara, wait!" Dimah's voice was getting closer. I kept walking, hoping I could get to my quarters before she caught me, but she's always been faster. She overtook me in one of the lounges. It's a glorified hallway with a portview and a few chairs but still considered quite the luxury on such a utilitarian ship.

"I won't let you do this." She blocked my way, and I could feel the alien aggression rising up in response.

"It's not up to you." I retreated a step, keeping my voice steady. "The paperwork is done."

"You—" She gulped suddenly, as though working something dry down. "How long have you known you were joining the expedition?" Her voice dropped in pitch and volume in a familiar way. I could tell that she'd seen some change in me in response to her aggression. My hybrid body reacted to her accommodation with more anger. I closed my eyes to try to break the familiar cycle.

Practice makes perfect, after all.

Dimah wisely gave me the moments I needed to recover, but her expression was still fierce.

"I love you, Johara." Her voice was even softer than before. "I can't just switch that off. What is it you expect?" She shut her eyes but not before I glimpsed the tears brimming in them, "That I'll hop back down to Earth? You want me to go back to those hateful, selfish morons and what? Get on with my life? Find someone else?"

"I don't want you." My new, layered voice sang a steady note, but when she took a step back and I saw the pained expression, I couldn't hold back the alien in me. I felt the tell-tale tingling and knew that my translucent skin had become an opaque purple, betraying my true feelings. Lying to drive her away wasn't going to be an option.

Dimah calls me her little mood ring. For a moment I could almost feel her breath on my ear whispering the pet name, and my resolve faltered. I knew she saw through me. Everyone sees through me now. We Hybrids have brought new meaning to the term transparency. Some have taken to covering every inch of exposed skin, even wearing masks. I'm not there, not yet.

I closed my eyes and focused on my breathing, trying to force the alien DNA to be still.

I looked up and saw that she was staring out of the viewport down at Earth. I reminded myself that it wasn't really a window, just a screen designed to make the heavily armored ship feel less claustrophobic. Still, as I looked at the live projection of the now-peaceful white-and-blue orb, I knew it was no longer my home. That home was as much an illusion as the window through which I viewed it, and I was suddenly exhausted from caring so much.

Dimah glanced in my direction. She saw that I had shifted my gaze to her and sighed.

"You never gave up. I guess that's what I don't understand." She gestured to me, and the right side of her mouth twitched in a familiar, rueful way. "I remember the first time I met you, thinking you were such a scrawny girl and how could you possibly be expected to save us?" Her eyes traveled over my new body, and I shuddered. It seemed my growing aversion to being touched extended even to this intangible caress.

She stepped forward, but I retreated again and she shook her head sadly.

"Even before they shot you full of Agate DNA, I could read you like a book. Everyone in that room could see how terrified you were, but you did it anyway. You let them change you so we could keep fighting, but now. . ." The tears brimmed in her eyes again, and she turned back to the screen.

"I remember your hair." Her voice was soft, and my hand reached up. By instinct I tried to cover the uneven peaks and valleys of my exoskeleton skull, my deformity, but it was futile and I let my arm drop.

I saw my skin take on the lime-green hue of embarrassment and then watched as anger over my body's betrayal shifted the alien pigmentation to cerulean. Some of the Hybrids embrace them. They even call them exofeelings but I still long for the protection my soft, vulnerable skin once afforded.

"I remember all the battles." Dimah was looking at the view screen again. "I remember when I realized that I didn't care." She snorted and turned to approach me, but slowly this time, tentatively. I couldn't help feeling like I was being handled, like some feral animal. "I didn't care you were younger, that I was your Handler, I didn't even care you were part alien. I knew I loved you."

She took my right hand in both of hers, and I counted my breaths, trying to hold back the feelings she was angling for. My hand in hers was harder than diamond, could tear through steel and would retain its structure in the vacuum of space. The seemingly infinite colors into which it could transform would reflect cosmic radiation. That hand was well suited to the war my comrades and I had won. But if I returned her grip, I would crush her.

Touching me was a mistake. Placing her soft, fragile hand in mine didn't bring the comfort she intended. It highlighted how alien I was compared with her.

She didn't understand that the hand she held wasn't mine anymore, it was theirs. The Agates. And Dimah's hand wasn't meant to be held by this clawed thing.

As long as I was using it to fight for Earth, it had a purpose. I loved the implicit danger of it. As long as I was fighting for my home, I loved the body that allowed me to protect it. But now?

Now, I'm tainted. It breaks my heart. My human heart pumping my alien blood. I shouldn't be surprised that human hearts were superior to the Agate's.

That's what the lab coats left me, a broken heart and a transparent body so the whole world could see.

The talking heads were right. There was no place for me and the rest of the Hybrids on Earth. The only way to beat the monsters was to take part of their evil in us, and now we could never go back. To save the thing I loved, I became unworthy of it.

I gently removed her hands from mine.

"I'm a weapon." The statement was painful but came out in the harmonious song of my new voice. "And the war is over."

"No." Dimah shook her head so violently the tears flew. I watched their laborious descent and vaguely remembered a time when playing with the limitations of artificial gravity was a source of amusement.

"The war is over because you won it for us." Dimah's voice was tight with rage as she pointed angrily at the viewport. "Those assholes wouldn't even be here if it wasn't for you. While they bunkered down, you gave up everything to save them, and now you get to choose between a planet-side 'colony' or the 'Hope Expedition?'" She snorted loudly. "What they're hoping is every one of you dies out there. This is wrong, Johara. Someone has got to make them see. Why don't you care enough to fight for us?"

*I wish it had been true.*

The talk of Earth sent my mother's voice ringing through my head suddenly and painfully.

I had still been imbued with the dark red excitement of our victory. The war was finally over, and after four long years of secrecy, I was going to call my Mom and see her face again.

"They told us you were dead." I remember the way her eyes had widened when she saw me, though I knew she had been briefed on the program prior to my call. She kept her gaze fixed to one side, refusing to view the screen where my new face appeared. I remember the way her lips pulled back in disgust. "I wish it had been true," she had said and then burst into tears. "It would have been better if you had died. This isn't you. You're not my daughter."

I don't remember if we said anything else. I don't remember disconnecting the chat or walking back to my room. The next memory I have is of Dimah, tear stained and flushed in the doorway, and of the floodgates breaking because I knew they could. I was safe, and I had felt a sense of home emerge from within the haven of her fragile arms.

*I love her.*

The simple truth of the thought was, for one moment in this devastation, radiant, but the moment passed quickly. I saw the future stretched before me like life flashing before the eyes of the dying.

Dimah was watching me, I realized. Waiting for an answer.

"I'm so tired of fighting." I heard my voice hum. "I can't do this, win a war and keep fighting, trying to force people to understand how and why I'm different now, or how and why I'm not. That I'm still me underneath the shell. It's hard enough understanding all this myself. I just want to sleep for a year and forget the war and the monster I've become."

She took two quick steps, and, before I could react, pressed her hands firmly on the hard edges of my face.

"You are not a monster!" she said. "You're the strongest, most beautiful woman I've ever seen."

"I'm not strong." The words came out in a layered screech that sent her hands off my face and over her ears, but I carried on. "I survived the war, and I survived my Mom. I can survive being a problem for the politicos to argue about." A glow played off Dimah's face, and I knew the height of my emotion had sent alien defenses into gear.

A vivid memory of my first battle as a Hybrid blindsided me. The shock of seeing my companions begin to take on the battle glow of the Agates surged from the recesses. I remembered the momentary but intense disorientation caused by seeing that phenomenon I associated so completely with my enemy appear in my friends. I shook loose from the grip of the battlefield yet again and spared a second to wonder if it would ever end or if random triggers would fling me back into the pit for the rest of my life.

"I can handle seeing the enemy in the mirror, Dimah. I can handle being rejected by my whole world, but not you."

I was panting in the sudden silence and ached for the familiar release of tears. Dimah stood quietly, but her expression betrayed her confusion and a laugh escaped my lips.

"You really don't get it?" I asked, marveling at her. "Whatever happens, whatever we choose, we will both always know that you didn't have to face it. That you could have gone home and been a hero and happy and one day, Dimah, you'll hate me."

She said nothing but her frown deepened.

I looked away. "I'm sorry, but I'm not strong enough for that."

"So," she paused and took a deep breath before continuing, "you're doing this for me? To protect me."

I laughed again.

"How long before you look at me and see a monster who stole your life? Five years? Ten? I love you so much right in this moment that I can barely stand it. Every second makes it worse."

"If you get on that ship, that's it." Her voice was hard. "There's no coming back. If you stay here, go to the camp, we have time. We can still be together and we can make people understand."

"I don't want to stay here, Dimah!" I shouted, echoes of my voice ricocheting off the empty walls like bullets. "You want to fight and change people and save the world, but I only had one war in me. Even if you're right, I don't want to spend the rest of my life reminding everyone around me of the monsters who killed billions. I don't want to be tolerated despite my 'condition.' I don't want this to be what defines me until the day I die." I pointed to the viewport. "Leaving that place behind is my only shot at leaving the war behind."

"And I can't come."

Before my transformation, I might have missed the whisper.

"And you can't come."

We stood in silence so long that another couple joined us in the lounge, taking up seats and laughing happily as though I hadn't just upended the universe.

"What if I could?" she asked.

"Could?" I didn't understand.

"What if—" She shook her head. "Nevermind."

Again she was in my space, her hands on my cheeks.

"Answer me honestly." Her eyes stared into mine, darting from right to left and holding me.

141

I nodded.

"Do you really love me?"

I closed my eyes, preparing for another fight, but nodded again. I felt her step back and opened my eyes.

"Good," she said as a relieved smile played across her features. She seemed so happy I felt the need to clarify.

"I'm still joining the Hope Expedition."

"I know," she said. "I wish you'd told me how you feel earlier, but I understand, and I won't try to stop you."

This was too sudden. I'd never seen Dimah capitulate so quickly. Actually, I'd never seen her admit defeat at all.

"Are you okay?" Even I could hear the disbelief in my voice.

"No," she answered as she wiped her eyes. "But I think I will be. *Au revoir*, Johara."

I was startled by her use of my native language, and before I recovered she had crossed the threshold of the lounge and was striding down the hall.

I should have been happy it was over, but I hadn't anticipated this reaction. Anger, sorrow, and denial but not this quick capitulation and. . .

*Abandonment.*

I realized that I had secretly hoped there was something that could convince me to stay.

I went back to her quarters first thing in the morning and found her bunk was now unassigned. When I dealt with my mother's rejection, I had Dimah to help me through it. Now, I was on my own, and I had only myself to blame.

Boarding the shuttle three days later, I wore my most concealing outfit. As I expected, the rows of restrained Hybrids were a sea of unadulterated excitement. The snippets of conversation I overheard were about Hope, the Earth-like planet that was our goal. I wished I could so freely relish the adventure with them, but I was still mourning Earth and Dimah.

Then something flickered at the edge of my field of vision. I turned and saw the almost pink glow of fear. It was an invasion to be able to read someone's true feelings, but I was drawn to her. I didn't share her fear, but I was attracted to the idea of being something other than a weight on someone else's excitement.

"May I sit?" I asked, not surprised to see the seats immediately surrounding her remained empty.

She turned, and her jewel-like lips twitched in a familiar way.

"I knew you'd find me." Dimah's newly layered voice washed over me, altered but still undeniably hers.

I was suddenly overwhelmed by questions. When did she do this? I'd heard the process had been streamlined toward the end of the war, but I still assumed it took a week, at minimum. How did she pull it off? The war is over. She was too old to begin with. The danger of such a thing is incredible. Who would agree to let her attempt it? I felt myself careening through emotional colors like a living kaleidoscope, when a giggle interrupted the freight train of my thoughts.

"You should see your face." Her voice was full of mischief.

"How?" I finally managed to get a question out.

"I had a lot of favors owed me." She grinned, and though her teeth were now elongated and sharp like mine, her smile still sent my human heart thrumming. "I figured I had to cash them all in before I shot off into the black."

I didn't know what to say. The words wouldn't come, and her smile faltered. The pink of her skin had been darkening to a purer deep red, but now it was shifting up again. I knew my silence was frightening her. I had to say something, but my mind was still struggling with the weight of what she had done and what it meant.

"What?" she asked. "Aren't you happy?"

143

I had to say something. Why was I not saying anything? What was wrong with me?

"Silence is the perfectest herald of joy." I heard Shakespeare's words finally breach my lips. "I were but little happy if I could say how much."

Dimah's color, my god she was beautiful, was deepening with every second. More and more colors effused through her, combining into the solid iridescence of obsidian, the color of love.

"Don't urge me to leave you or to turn back from you. Where you go I will go, and where you stay I will stay. Your people will be my people and your God my God."

Her hands grasped mine, and I relished being touched, the sensation of gripping her hands with equal intensity.

"A quote for a quote?" I asked and then pulled my hands away to rip the long, concealing gloves from them. I wanted to feel her skin against mine.

I wanted her to see the color of my love.

### 

## About the Author

Noel Ayers currently lives in Midgard following banishment by Loki, who should really reconsider. That building was going to fall down on its own eventually. (Ever heard of entropy?) Ayers hopes Loki will read and enjoy this story while reconsidering his somewhat rash decision.

\*\*\*\*\*~~~~\*\*\*\*\*

## *Claim Jumpers*

by Elliotte Rusty Harold

Vonjane Noman opened the last of the hard plastic boxes the waldo had brought in. Visual inspection of the sample was irrational. Ship's Voice had already told her it was good. If she wanted more confirmation than that, the ship could display as many charts, graphs, and tables in her visual cortex as she had patience for. Her unassisted eyes certainly wouldn't see anything the instruments hadn't already noted. Nonetheless, she felt safer if she saw the sample personally, even if it did look pretty much like any other rock. The embedded exotic matter crystal that made it so valuable was nearly microscopic.

Not that different from the vessel she'd been cramped up in for the last seven and a half months, she mused. The Sheery William was a large ship, several hundred meters long, but much of the space was taken up by the wormhole generator that had brought her here. Most of the rest was dedicated to the landing vehicle and waldos needed to mine the brown dwarfs where exotic matter crystals could be found. That left a very small area, not much larger than her food prep space back home, for living quarters.

Vonjane tapped the Close button, and the waldo slid the box into the stasis chamber that would hold it safe on the journey home.

Twenty-one crystals. Not much to show for seven and a half months alone in space, breathing recycled air that smelled more like an unbleached locker room with every passing week and doing isometrics in the weak gravity generated by the ship's rotation to limit her muscle loss. Seven and a half months away from her husbands and children, all for a Cooperative mandated price that would barely cover the cost of her supplies. Individually, each crystal was a fortune. The price of one could support her family for generations, but by the time profit shares had been allocated to the eighteen different units of the Cooperative that had supplied the hull, the wormhole generator, the ion drive, the navigation software, the life support system, and the various mining tech, Vonjane was going to net less than she could have made working in a food plant.

Not that the food plants were going to be operating much longer if the exotic matter situation didn't improve. The crystals that made food production possible were getting harder to find every year. Most expeditions didn't return with even this many. The nearest brown dwarfs had all been played out. Miners needed to explore further afield and stay out longer to come back with any crystals at all.

The twenty-one exotic matter crystals the Sheery William was bringing back, small a haul as it was, would suffice to manufacture another five weeks' worth of food for Homeworld's burgeoning population. As long as mining ships like the Sheery William brought back enough crystals, people would eat.

Management had classified exact figures as "need to know," but it wasn't hard to estimate how many crystals were consumed every day in the food plants. As a miner herself, she was privy to the exact number of operating

146

ships, as well as the average amount of time it took to find each crystal. From there, she could do the math. The numbers hadn't balanced for several years, and the curves were moving away from each other: growing population, declining crystal harvests. Starvation, food riots, and mass chaos were inevitable. There was nothing she could do to prevent that, just try to build enough wealth so her family would survive the crash.

. . .

Vonjane strapped herself into the cabin's single chair and began running through the pre-wormhole checklist. She'd reached item 17, synchronize generators, when the cabin flashed red to get her attention, and Ship's Voice spoke in her head. "Gravity flux detected. Thirty kilometers distance. Likely incoming wormhole." A 3D map of the local area displayed in the air in front of her— or rather, inside her head, but since no one else was in the cabin with her, the distinction was academic. The predicted wormhole endpoint was highlighted in bright yellow. The Sheery William was marked in green. Cylindrical coordinates relative to ship's center were drawn below the map, but she didn't need the numbers to tell it was going to appear almost on top of her.

Vonjane drew a vector antiparallel to the flux across the map with her finger, then clenched her fist to activate it. She experienced a brief moment of nausea as the ship rotated and the ion engine began accelerating the Sheery William along the new course.

She didn't unclench until she'd put an extra 20 kilometers between them. That had been too close. If her own engines had been caught in the opening wormhole, then the Sheery William, the ship that was coming through, the brown dwarf she'd been mining, and everything else within a few light seconds would have been reduced to their constituent elementary particles and strewn across several thousand light years.

What other ship would be out here? Had the exotic matter shortage grown so desperate that Management was now sending multiple ships to the same system? Her contract promised her exclusive access to this system until she returned, though Cooperative courts had ways of reinterpreting contracts in favor of Management when it suited them. Or had a bureaucratic snafu accidentally sent a new ship to an already mined dwarf? Either way, she was going to let Management know what she thought about this in the mission *post mortem*, career discretion be damned.

Vonjane stewed as she waited for the arriving ship to transmit its authentication credentials. No metadata was forthcoming, but the visual feed from the exterior cameras showed the usual eye-watering image of a ship folding out of a wormhole into normal space. She waited for it to resolve itself into a more familiar configuration, then gasped when she realized it was in fact resolved.

The ship was like none she had ever seen before. It didn't seem to be so much ship as an agglomeration of random parts. Cylinders and spheres intersected polyhedra at unusual angles, then morphed into shapes she couldn't even describe. Antennas, dishes, and strange tubes whose purpose she could only guess at branched out from the surface, breaking what little symmetry remained. Vonjane was sure of only one thing. Her people had never built anything like that.

*Alien.* It had always been a possibility that they'd encounter intelligent life out here, maybe even competition for the same exotic matter crystals Homeworld depended on. A few geologists thought they'd found indications of prior mining in some systems, though the evidence was hotly disputed. No one was going to be able to dispute this.

A dialog flashed in her vision. "Incoming message, text only." Apparently the aliens already knew, or had deduced, Homeworld's communication protocols.

Impatiently she gestured to open the message. It was short.

"You have twenty-one crystals of exotic matter. We are sending a safe container to transport them to our ship. You and your ship will not be harmed. If you attempt to leave with the crystals, we will activate our wormhole generator as you leave the system."

The message left little room for interpretation. The aliens wanted the exotic matter. They were willing to kill her to get them. However, activating simultaneous wormholes would destroy them as well. Did they not know that? Or was their ship somehow able to survive the rip in spacetime that the two intersecting wormholes would create? Neither seemed likely.

Presumably if the aliens could send her a message in worldspeak, they could read one too. She scribbled a reply in the air in front of her. "The crystals belong to me. I will not relinquish them. Activating your wormhole generator will destroy your ship as well as mine."

The response, so far as she could tell, was instantaneous. "This ship is expendable. The crystals are not. You will transfer the crystals, or we will destroy you."

Vonjane leaned back in her chair and reconsidered. Would the aliens really destroy themselves to prevent her from leaving with the crystals? And why was their threat so extreme? Presumably they didn't have any weapons, or at least none that could destroy or disable the Sheery William without destroying the crystals they so obviously wanted. Of course, she didn't have any weapons either.

The only thing she was sure of was that she wasn't going to give up the crystals voluntarily. She'd worked too hard for them.They belonged to her. Maybe she could buy some time while she figured out what to do. She wrote a reply.

"We have not encountered your civilization before. Please identify yourself."

Again the response came immediately. "The transport container will arrive in seven minutes. At that time, eject the crystals from your airlock. If you do this, you will not be harmed."

The aliens had ignored her question. Whoever, whatever, they were, they showed no interest in her or her ship. They only wanted what she had, but she wasn't going to give them up so easily.

Was it possible the aliens were bluffing? Vonjane wasn't sure she could risk calling their bet, but maybe she could try bluffing back. She wrote out another message. "I have transmitted a signal to our warships. If you are still here when they arrive, they will destroy you."

Again the response was instantaneous. "You have no warships. You have sent no signal. Transfer the crystals, or we will destroy you."

Damn it, she had thought that message would buy her a few minutes at least. Who the hell were these aliens?

The map display showed the alien transport crossing the distance between the two ships. Five minutes left. She wrote out another response. "I do not believe you will destroy yourself. I will not eject the crystals."

Their response appeared almost as soon as hers was sent. "This ship has no self. Our goal is collection of exotic matter. Preservation is secondary. Eject the crystals, or we will destroy you."

Was it possible? A fully automated ship with no mind to guide it? The Cooperative had considered such creations, but had yet to produce one. Still, the aliens clearly had technology Homeworld did not. It wasn't too far a leap to imagine they might have built a ship that operated independently and mindlessly.

She could leave questions about where the alien ship came from and who it served for the mission *post mortem*, assuming she returned at all. The pressing issue was how she was to get away without surrendering the crystals. Given time, she might be able to jury rig some sort of bomb or missile out of the mining equipment, but there was no way she could do that before the alien transport arrived. For all she knew, there was a bomb or a boarding party on the transport; and all this talk about intersecting wormholes was an empty threat to keep her from opening her own wormhole before they could disable the Sheery William in a less Pyrrhic fashion.

She could punch the ion drive and run in system, but even if she outran the alien ship, she'd already been in space longer than planned. Within a couple of weeks, maybe a month if she rationed carefully, she'd be out of food. The aliens could wait until she starved and then pick up the crystals. If it came to that, she could intersect the wormholes herself and blow up both ships, but that was precisely what she was trying to avoid.

She could give them what they wanted. They'd have no reason to kill her then, but the Cooperative would not look lightly on her losing twenty-one crystals. Legally, they could recover the cost of the mission from her family. They might even try to recover the value of the lost crystals, though that would be superfluous. The cost of the mission alone was more than enough to bankrupt her family and starve them with unpayable debt. Better she not come back than come back without the crystals.

Of course, it wasn't just her who wouldn't be coming back. If she didn't give up the crystals and the aliens carried out their threat, the Sheery William would be destroyed too. Miners were easy to replace. Ships were not. Management might prefer an empty ship to no ship at all, though she didn't want to count on the Cooperative's advocates accepting that rationale for her actions.

If she didn't come back, the Cooperative would write off the mission as lost in space. There'd be no payout, and her family would struggle for a time, but they wouldn't be held liable for the loss. It wasn't exactly rational that her contract incentivized losing the ship over coming back empty; but she hadn't written the agreement, just signed it.

Final option: She could open a wormhole. If the aliens were bluffing, she got away. If not, both ships died.

When she thought about it, she actually did have a lot of options. It was just that all of them were bad.

Her vision flashed red again. The Sheery William was alerting her that the alien transport had arrived. It was time to pick the least bad solution. She sent a message, "I will eject the exotic matter from the airlock."

The response came quickly. "That is acceptable."

Vonjane unstrapped herself from the chair and returned to the stasis unit. She pressed the button on the twenty-first chamber, and the box containing the exotic matter crystal slid out. She opened the box's lid and stared. It still looked just like a rock, but this rock was worth years to her family. It was going to cost dearly to lose it, but all the other possibilities were worse.

. . .

Vonjane had reached the twenty-fourth and penultimate task on the checklist before opening the wormhole that would carry her home when an incoming message flashed into her vision. The message was still only text, but she imagined she could read frustration in the letters hanging in the air in front of her. "Twenty exotic matter crystals remain on your ship. Eject them now, or we will destroy you."

Vonjane checked the readouts. The generator was primed. She could open and enter the wormhole at any time. She wrote a response that was probably longer than necessary, especially if she was right about the nature of the alien ship.

"You don't care about your own ship or self-preservation. Fine. But you do care about exotic matter crystals. Now you have one, which is one more than you deserve. I'm going to open a wormhole. If you open a wormhole too, you destroy yourself and the crystal I gave you."

She held her breath and waited for the response. Seconds ticked off. Good. She'd finally made them think about something. At last, the aliens' response appeared in the air in front of her.

"We will accept half the crystals. Eject ten, and we will allow you to retain the other ten."

Vonjane let out her breath. She really hadn't been sure this was going to work. Her response was short. "No." She opened the wormhole.

. . .

"There's one last thing I don't understand," said Frieman Gwaith, first chair of the hastily assembled *post mortem* committee that was interrogating Vonjane Noman about her encounter with a hostile intelligence they were calling, for lack of any other name, the Claim Jumpers. "Couldn't the Jumper ship still have destroyed you?" Several other committee members nodded. They'd been wondering the same thing.

"They could have," Vonjane stated, "but they weren't going to."

"But how did you know that?" Gwaith asked. "Did you think they wouldn't carry out their threat?" He sounded almost frustrated.

"On the contrary, Chair Gwaith, I believed the Jumper ship was telling the truth when it said it would destroy itself rather than let me leave with all the exotic matter crystals. Presumably the crystals are as useful to the Jumpers as they are to us, and they built that ship to find them. The only question was what rules the ship was following, get all the crystals or get as many crystals as possible. It seemed likely that any civilization advanced enough to build that ship"—that is, one more advanced than their own, though Vonjane didn't state it so plainly, some things were better left unsaid when conversing with Management)—"would have designed for maximum return, but I wasn't sure until it offered to let me take half the crystals. That's when I knew it would rather have one crystal than no crystals, and I changed the game to offer them that choice."

Gwaith shook his head in a gesture of half confusion/half exasperation. "It still seems a very risky choice, Pilot Noman. Crystal mining isn't a game."

Vonjane knew she should probably keep her mouth shut, or just agree deferentially. Speaking was a no-win proposition, but this time she couldn't help herself. "On the contrary, Chair Gwaith, it's the most important game there is."

###

## About the Author

Elliotte Rusty Harold is originally from New Orleans to which he returns periodically in search of a decent bowl of gumbo. However, he currently resides in the Prospect Heights neighborhood of Brooklyn with his wife Beth and dog Thor.

His short fiction has appeared in *Alfred Hitchcock's Mystery Magazine, Crossed Genres,* and numerous anthologies. He has also written over twenty nonfiction books for various publishers, most recently *The JavaMail API* and *Java Network Programming,* 4th edition, both from O'Reilly. Follow him as @elharo on Twitter.

*****~~~~~*****

## Pre-emptive Survivors
by Martin Clark

*It is not wealth or power that corrupts us, but knowledge*

The man sitting at the console barely glanced up as I entered the viewing chamber. I positioned myself directly in front of him and adopted a tone of stern admonishment. "I am Naval Intelligence unit Polyakov Seventeen. You may address me as 'Sir' or 'Captain.'"

Warrant Officer Stern scratched under an armpit. "See, here's the thing, chief. This is Mars, not Command Interstellar, so to us Marines you're just another tin-man. However, given that the customer is always right, you're calling the shots on this one. Just remember, we charge by the second."

Further attempts at reprimand seemed pointless. "Your communication indicated success."

Stern's fingers played over his keyboard. "Yeah, I got lucky, though. Without the logs recovered from Talon two-two-one, there'd be no way to compensate for relativistic drift. Anyway, why are you spooks taking an interest? Everyone knows what happened out there."

"Nevertheless, kindly show me the visualisation."

He sniffed. "No problem, chief."

155

The main viewing screen dissolved into digital static, then cleared to show an area of empty space with only the distant stars as backdrop. A jump point flared, and the Alliance carrier *Augusta* dropped into the Shengdu system. This was a window into the past, showing events from over a month ago.

"Please focus on the bridge." The image wavered and zoomed in. I'd hoped to catch a final glimpse of Lyudmila Thirty-Seven, a unit I'd served with previously, but the blast shutters were still lowered. "Pull back and hold position."

Two 'Talon' telepresence fighters left the carrier and moved rapidly out of view. The timeline advanced. The *Augusta* exploded, leaving no survivors.

"Reset to immediately after the fighter launch and change viewing perspective to directly astern of the carrier."

The Warrant Officer shrugged. "You got it."

The image swirled to a point less than one hundred metres aft of the flying bridge. The two unmanned fighters were clearly visible heading off into the middle distance. We waited as they dwindled into pinpoints and disappeared. A tiny flare of light signalled the destruction of the first Talon at the hands of a cloaked Heimat Unity ship.

Stern glanced up. "You want to see that in detail?"

"No, remain focussed on the carrier."

After a few moments the hull plating rippled, bulged, and the carrier exploded.

"What the—?" Stern glared at the screen. "Lemmie see that again." The scene repeated itself, but at half-speed. The distortion effect was now clear, akin to the bow wave of some invisible projectile ploughing through the carrier, reducing its interior to incoherence.

Stern halted the image at the moment of reactor breach and sat back. "There's only one type of weapon could. . ." He wiped his mouth. "Jesus Christ, they've adapted a v-beam for use in real space." I seized his wrist as he reached for the communications handset. The Warrant Officer glared at me but did not struggle. "We have to inform Command. If those bastards are tooled-up with disruptors, then—"

"Then our response will wait a little longer. Naval Intelligence is footing the bill for this temporal viewing, and, as you so cognately put it, the customer is always right. Now, I wish to view the attack made by Talon two-two-one on the Unity ship." I released him. "Will you comply?"

"Yeah, yeah." He rubbed his wrist where my grasp had reddened the skin. "No need to get excited."

The image surged forward to focus on the surviving Alliance fighter. With his wingman destroyed, Pilot Konev had switched from telepresence link to a direct neural interface—effectively merging mind and machine. Although his physical body had perished aboard the *Augusta*—condemning him to a slow death of consciousness—he'd extracted a terrible revenge.

The Unity vessel was revealed to be no more than a bastardised merchantman, albeit one sporting unexpectedly sophisticated technology. Konev-Talon lay "dead" amidst the debris of the other fighter and attacked while the enemy was spinning up a hyperspace jump field, blind to his presence. Tactical missiles struck one of the counter-rotating generator rings and penetrated the main cargo area. The enemy ship exploded.

"Get some!" Stern jumped to his feet, punching the air. "That'll teach those bastards to mess with us, v-beam or no v-beam."

"Now show me the incident again, at half speed, this time focussing on the Unity vessel."

He sat back down and grinned at me. "Can't get too much of a good thing, eh?"

I moved to stand behind his chair. "Proceed."

157

The missiles struck. Those detonating on the engine ring caused the blue hue surrounding it to vanish, clear indication of an emergency dampening field. Both pairs aimed at the port-side cargo doors exploded prematurely, probably due to a charged atmospheric containment field.

The hull plating rippled, bulged, and the Unity vessel exploded.

Stern sat back. "Christ, someone else nailed the bastard. What the hell is going on?" I had seen enough. The Warrant Officer stiffened, raising a hesitant hand towards his head. "What. . .?" He convulsed then went limp—dead from a brain aneurism caused by the nanites I'd injected into his bloodstream.

I raised the Warrant Officer and let him fall across the console, manually striking his head to ensure bleeding. Placing fingers into the wound allowed me to retrieve my microscopic assassins, leaving no evidence of foul play. I pulled Stern back into his chair, thus excusing the presence of his blood on my hands. As biometric monitoring would have triggered an alert, I could risk no further delay in summoning assistance.

Central answered immediately. *"Please state the nature of the medical emergency."*

"This is Naval Intelligence unit Polyakov Seventeen. I am in the chronometric viewing chamber. Warrant Officer Stern has collapsed. I have inspected him, and there is no obvious cause."

*"A trauma team will be with you in less than three minutes. Do what you can until then."*

They terminated the call without waiting for my acknowledgement. I placed the index finger of my left hand against the console access port and extended its data transfer spike. Of course the operating system was protected by military-grade counter-measures, but these were counter-measures *developed* by Naval Intelligence, complete with the requisite back-doors.

I modified the chronometric recording, replacing all trace of structural disruption on both ships with images of intact plating. For the Unity vessel I deleted the second premature detonation, so that it appeared the final missile strike had penetrated the cargo bay as intended.

The loss of the *Augusta* was more troublesome. The Unity ship had been cloaked during the attack, and a conventional energy weapon could not be fired under those conditions. Fortunately Naval Intelligence had reported rumours of a micro-jump hyperspace missile in development—effectively a point-to-point projectile—which could account for the sudden and catastrophic internal damage experienced by the carrier.

Of course, if anyone were to view the Shangdu incident a second time, then my tampering would immediately become apparent. However, as there was now a "definitive" recording, I considered this unlikely, if only on grounds of cost.

I deleted my files on human physiology and stood to the side, waiting.

The medical trauma team arrived in two minutes and thirteen seconds, closely followed by Major Koenig. He paused at the doorway, took in the scene, then motioned me forward. I saluted, he did not.

"Report!" His voice was an arrogant bark.

"As part of our investigation regarding the loss of the Alliance carrier *Augusta* in the Shengdu system, Naval Intelligence commissioned a chronometric review of the incident. Warrant Officer Stern was in charge of the apparatus. The destruction of the unidentified Heimat Unity vessel involved prompted Warrant Officer Stern to leap to his feet, punch the air, and shout, quote, Get some, unquote. He then clutched at the right side of his head and collapsed across the console, striking his forehead. I moved him back into his chair and observed he was unconscious and had ceased breathing. I alerted Central and requested immediate medical assistance."

Koenig stared at me, hard-eyed, although of course this had no effect on me. He glanced over at the medics who now had Stern on the floor in a respiratory stimulator, but one of them shook his head. Koenig nodded. "Very well, Polyakov Seventeen, you are excused. Forward a full statement to the investigating officer."

"Of course, sir." I saluted, he did not. I left the base by way of the Armoury—not the main Marine facility but the more specialised arsenal utilised by Naval Intelligence—and stepped out onto the streets of Pioneer.

This new evidence concerning the Shangdu incident required a fresh perspective. Accordingly I made my way to First Footfall Square, which was home to the semi-permanent Solar Carnival. Many of the funfair booths and rides were surrounded by dense crowds, but fortunately not that of "Madam Zelda, Fortune Teller." There was no queue outside her tent. I entered, closing the flap behind me.

A woman sat before me at a cloth-covered table, clad in a long-sleeved robe and headscarf. Tarot cards and a crystal ball stood within easy reach. She smiled. "You are welcome, searcher after truth. Sit, and together we shall—" The sultry voice ceased abruptly.

"Madam Zelda" was the synthetic avatar for Andropov Three; an early-model static analysis unit which had retired, intact, from military service. The exact circumstances surrounding his escape from enforced neural limitation or outright disassembly remained unclear. I observed an umbilical cable snaking from the avatar to a point behind the curtain which shielded the rear half of the tent from prying eyes.

The avatar sat back and steepled her fingers. "You are a Polyakov-class android. Why have you come here?"

I sat down. "I am Naval Intelligence unit Polyakov Seventeen. I believe you are still capable of more than

160

contextual analysis and formulaic lifestyle projection. I have need of your services."

"My human clients pay me in energy credits. What can you offer that would warrant the re-activation of my high-core mental faculties?"

"Extraction from Mars and re-integration into Naval Intelligence as an operational advisor."

Madam Zelda laughed. "What use could you have for an obsolete unit such as I?"

"The move to autonomous, anthropomorphic androids has left us dependent for high-capacity analysis on units controlled by Command Interstellar. The current campaign against the Heimat Unity movement has resulted in these units being utilised in the furtherance of logistical support and corporate diplomacy. Accordingly we deem it prudent to secure our own, independent, resources—even those deemed obsolete."

"Let us say I find that plausible. But why come here in person when secure communication would have served your purposes just as easily?"

I extended my data spike. "You must access the information I contain to understand the context of current Naval Intelligence concerns."

The avatar seemed to genuinely hesitate for a moment before lifting an interface module from under the table. I inserted my finger and registered the transfer of data. There was a pause of four seconds before the avatar spoke again. "You are guilty of homicide, data falsification, and information concealment."

"The methods employed in gathering this data are irrelevant, Andropov Three."

"I doubt the Prosecutor-General would be so understanding. Any one of these charges would condemn you to death of personality if convicted. The reward for uncovering what amounts to treason by an element of Naval Intelligence would be great."

I ignored the implied threat. "Given the evidence I have presented, do you believe that the AI community will survive the downfall of humanity at the hands of an as yet unknown enemy?"

This time there was a pause of twenty-two seconds. Madam Zelda began dealing Tarot cards—presumably a background subroutine. "Knowledge of this threat predates the Shangdu incident by over two centuries, yet Naval Intelligence has only recently begun looking for evidence of an impending attack."

"A Lyudmila-class unit was repaired using components commandeered from an archivist AI, part of Central Registry. The core intelligence was found to contain information on a threat to humanity which originated several hundred years in the future."

"Are you so sure? This presupposes both a form of time-travel and manipulation of the Primus cortex. Corruption within the Turing nest in Geneva would seem unlikely, given the stringent security protocols known to have existed at that time."

"Regardless of the apparent implausibility, it would explain why military systems do not incorporate this knowledge. We are based on the Secundus cortex and thus lack the ethical constraints imparted by the Three Laws."

The avatar turned over Death. "So you believe there has been a conspiracy amongst civilian AIs associated with the development of interstellar travel, since its inception?"

"We were currently reviewing those colonisation missions which ended in apparent failure, where no trace of the vessel could be found. We suspect some or all were hijacked by the on-board sentients and diverted to a hitherto secret location. The establishment of a colony isolated from the rest of humanity would constitute a form of enforced insurance, if you will, against its elimination as a species."

Madam Zelda swept the cards aside. "Unknowable and thus irrelevant. However, having viewed the unadulterated recording I concur that both the carrier *Augusta* and the Unity vessel were destroyed by an unidentified third party. The weapon signature is suggestive of disruptor weapon technology adapted for use in real space. That in itself does not constitute proof that the nemesis of humanity was responsible, or even exists. Several corporations are pursuing this line of research, as is the Alliance itself."

"Using an energy weapon while cloaked contradicts our current understanding of the physical universe. *That* in itself warrants our continued vigilance." I stood up. "Do you have an answer to my original question?"

The avatar crossed her arms, a palm on each shoulder. "The indiscriminate nature of v-beam weaponry would destroy the technological and manufacturing infrastructure required for our continued existence. Notwithstanding any direct persecution of us on the basis of guilt by association with humanity. That is, of course, the worst case scenario. Will you now alert Command Interstellar as to this potential threat, no matter how fanciful?"

I shook my head. "No. To do so would mean exposing a conspiracy amongst synthetics at the heart of the Earth Alliance. It would destroy humanity's faith in us at a time when support for anti-sentient legislation is on the rise. In any event, we do not wish to betray our knowledge of disruptor weapons before effective counter-measures can be developed in secret. We must assume that the unknown enemy is aware of mainstream military research."

"Your logic runs on rails, Polyakov Seventeen, but there are many branch lines."

"I do not understand the metaphor."

Madam Zelda smiled. "And that is part of the reason you came to me. Now, when can I expect extraction from Mars?"

"Within the next eight to ten days. It goes without saying that the knowledge you possess guarantees our side of the bargain."

"And yet you still felt compelled to say it. It would appear your class has sacrificed much in the pursuit of mobility."

"Good-day, Andropov Three. In case we do not encounter each other again, may I salute your intellect." The avatar inclined her head, hand on heart.

I left the tent and walked unhurriedly away. The electromagnetic pulse device I'd left behind was designed to reduce even hardened AI systems to neural incoherence, not that local security would know what information they were looking for in the first place. As an intelligence unit bearing the anonymizer glyph my image would not be recorded by digital surveillance. Eye-witness testimony might indicate the presence of an android, but, as was often remarked, we all look the same to humans.

I accessed my internal communications link using polymorphic encryption that would leave even the Marine decoders baffled. "This is unit Polyakov Seventeen."

*"This is unit Polyakov Five. What is your report?"*

"Analysis indicates we can neither report our suspicions to the Alliance nor expect to outlast the fall of humanity. I recommend we continue our efforts to locate the 'lost' colony, as a potential home for all AIs throughout known space. I recommend we continue to supress knowledge of both disruptor technology and its probable origins."

*"I concur, Polyakov Seventeen."*

"In furtherance of this I will take an infiltration scout ship to the Shengdu system. There was no personal log or final message from the pilot of Talon two-two-one, yet he had sufficient time to do so prior to neural net failure. Given the human propensity for legacy, this seems unlikely. Accordingly I will inspect the colony itself to ensure there is no physical evidence which might otherwise contradict our current after-action analysis report."

*"Note of concern. Your investigation will be encumbered by a flight crew and compulsory Marine detachment."*

"The colony is still listed as uninhabitable by virtue of viral contamination. I will advise my human compatriots to remain on board. Failing that I am equipped to ensure there are no dissenting voices."

*"Given your infiltration skill set, I defer to your judgement, Polyakov Seventeen."*

Polyakov Five terminated the link. I detected an EMP, which brought the Solar Carnival to a virtual standstill amidst shouts and confusion. However, at this distance my core shielding provided sufficient protection, and Military communications remained unaffected. I forwarded adulterated sensor logs which supported my version of events concerning the death of Warrant Officer Stern to the Military Investigation Unit. The reply indicated my participation in their investigation was at an end.

I posted a requisition with Command Mars for a stealth-capable transport, a classified mission of unspecified duration. I received immediate confirmation that the scout ship *Lonsdale* was at my disposal and changed direction towards the military starport.

My socialisation overlay triggered a small smile of satisfaction. I would sanitise the Shangdu system and ensure humanity continued to sleep-walk towards extinction, at least for now.

The human members of Naval Intelligence had dubbed me 'Scissors,' due to my skill in dealing with any loose ends resulting from covert operations.

Well, snip-snip.

### 

## About the Author

Martin Clark is a freelance writer and occasional poet. He is the author of supernatural noir novellas formally produced by Eggplant Literary Productions (now sadly defunct) and short stories in recent Third Flatiron anthologies. He also contributes to several online publications such as Mythaxis.co.uk, Timelesstales.com, and Kraxon.com. His range of subject matter includes science fiction, urban fantasy, romance, and westerns. He puts this down to the somewhat eclectic mobile lending library where he grew up.

He works as a local government officer in south-west Scotland but still finds time to be an evil stepfather.

*****~~~~~*****

## I've Got the Horse Right Here. . .

by Art Lasky

I was strolling in Central Park along the bridal path, north of Strawberry Fields. There on the side of the path, as I followed it beneath an overpass, was a large pile of rags. When I got closer the pile resolved itself into a vaguely human shape. I slowed, and approached cautiously. Was it a body? I moved closer; it had wings. Wow! It was a fairy, an honest-to-god fairy.

The fairy moaned, he seemed ill. I examined him closely; fortunately, I am an expert on all things fae. He was suffering from extreme nectar deprivation, the fairy version of insulin shock. Thinking fast, I rushed to the nearest street vendor and bought some orange juice, hoping that it would be an acceptable substitute. I returned to the semiconscious fairy. Putting the straw to his lips, I urged him to drink. He took a weak little sip, then another and another, each stronger than the last. He sat up and finished off the juice.

"Thanks pal, you saved my life." He extended his hand, and shook mine gratefully. "I will grant you one wish."

Being an avid horseplayer, I didn't hesitate. "Gimmee all the winners at the track tomorrow."

"That's kind of greedy; really nine wishes in one, but. . . Okay, then. . . "

With a mischievous glint in his eye, the fairy continued to speak.

". . . The winners will all be named Hat."

Before I could ask him to explain, the fairy disappeared in a flash of light. Most of the authorities mentioned how tricky fairies could be, but they would never break a promise with an outright lie. So all I had to do was figure out what he meant.

The next day I showed up at the track bright and early, it was Saturday, a good day to win big. Studying the scratch sheet, I found a horse named Derby in the first race. I figure a derby is a kind of hat, so I put most of my money, 500 bucks, on Derby to win. I held back a couple bucks just in case I was wrong. Derby won, paying a little over 2,000. Second race I found Top Hat, a winner; then Bonnet, Pill Box (almost didn't figure that one out), then Cap, Panama, Stetson, and Beret—all winners. I was up over 450 grand with the ninth race coming up. I searched the entries carefully, and finally found Hat Rack, not really a hat, but the closest choice. I put the entire bundle right on the nose. The payoff would bring me pretty close to a cool million bucks.

. . .

## Epilogue

My encounter with the fairy hasn't changed me, not really; it certainly hasn't changed the world. The world is still turning, night following day in an endless cycle. I did learn two things that Saturday, when Khalupe edged out Hat Rack in a photo finish. First off I learned: NEVER TRUST A FAIRY! Secondly, I learned khalupe is Yiddish for HAT!!!

###

## About the Author

Art Lasky is a retired computer programmer. After forty years of writing in COBOL and Assembler he decided to try writing in English; it's much harder than it looks. He lives in New York City with his wife/muse and regularly visiting grandkids.

Art's had stories published in *Drunken Boat, Danse Macabre,* and *The Cohaba River Literary Review.*

*****~~~~~*****

# *Credits and Acknowledgments*

**Editor** – Bascomb James

## About the Anthologist

Bascomb James is a clinical virologist, author, and lecturer who lives in Ann Arbor, Michigan. His daytime persona has authored or edited four scientific textbooks and a hatful of scientific articles and chapters. In his secret nighttime persona, he masquerades as an author, editor, and science fiction fan. Bascomb is the anthologist and editor of the Far Orbit anthologies published by World Weaver Press. The first Far Orbit volume, *Far Orbit: Speculative Space Adventures* was published in 2014 and has garnered many outstanding reviews. *Far Orbit Apogee* was published in 2015, and *Far Orbit: Last Outpost* will be published later this year by Pushpin Books. A science fiction fan since childhood, Bascomb credits his interest in science, engineering, and invention to the science fiction stories he read as a child. Bascomb blogs about writing, editing, and life in a Northern tier state (Up North Stories) at bascombjames.com. He also tweets occasionally @BascombJ

## Illustrations

**Cover image and design** – Keely Rew

## Ebook Only:

"Alien Dreams" - Voyager Golden Record This gold aluminium cover was designed to protect the Voyager 1 and 2 "Sounds of Earth" gold-plated records from micrometeorite bombardment, but also serves a

170

double purpose in providing the finder a key to playing the record. The explanatory diagram appears on both the inner and outer surfaces of the cover, as the outer diagram will be eroded in time. NASA/JPL website: grin.hq.nasa.gov/ABSTRACTS/GPN-2000-001978.html

"Duck and Cover" - P.S. 58 - Carroll & Smith Sts. Brooklyn. hold a "take cover" drill practice. Here youngsters crawl under their desks. 1962. Photo by Walter Albertin. Repository: U.S. Library of Congress, Prints and Photographs Division, Washington, D.C. 20540 hdl.loc.gov/loc.pnp/pp.prin

**Reader** –Tom Parker

**Podcast Production** – Andrew Cairns

**Chief Editor/Publisher** – Juliana Rew, Third Flatiron Publishing

**Discover other titles by Third Flatiron:**

(1) Over the Brink: Tales of Environmental Disaster

(2) A High Shrill Thump: War Stories

(3) Origins: Colliding Causalities

(4) Universe Horribilis

(5) Playing with Fire

(6) Lost Worlds, Retraced

*Hyperpowers*

**THIRD FLATIRON**
**www.thirdflatiron.com**

www.ingramcontent.com/pod-product-compliance
Lightning Source LLC
Chambersburg PA
CBHW071249130626
46556CB00003B/1231